THE GREAT
TURKEY
WALK

THE GREAT
TURKEY
WALK

Kathleen Karr

A Sunburst Book

Farrar, Straus and Giroux

Library of Congress Cataloging-in-Publication Data
Karr, Kathleen.
   The great turkey walk / Kathleen Karr. — 1st ed.
      p.   cm.
   Summary: In 1860, a somewhat simple-minded fifteen-year-old
boy attempts to herd one thousand turkeys from Missouri to Denver,
Colorado, in hopes of selling them at a profit.
   ISBN 0-374-42798-4 (pbk.)
   [1. Turkeys—Fiction.   2. West (U.S.)—Fiction.]   I. Title.
PZ7.K149Gr   1998
[Fic]—dc21   97-38859

For Elaine Chubb
copy editor *par excellence*

THE GREAT
TURKEY
WALK

❦ ONE ❦

I've always been fond of birds, poultry in particular. Maybe that's on account of the fact that Aunt Maybelle took to calling me *pea-brained* fairly early on. That's as in peahen, or peafowl.

Now, I know for a fact that was meant as an insult, considering the size of most birds' brains. Small. Tiny. Hardly there at all. I never took it as such, though. Trotted off to the schoolmarm instead, first time I heard the epithet. Miss Rogers, she just pulled out her worn copy of Webster's—that's the best dictionary in these United States—and showed me that peafowl were really *peacocks*.

"Well!" I strutted around the schoolroom. *"Peacocks* are some gorgeous birds, ain't they, Miss Rogers?"

Miss Rogers smiled. "They do make up in elegance what they lack in intelligence, Simon," she answered.

Miss Rogers always talked like that. She was an elegant lady all around. Not that I considered myself *that* elegant. Or that I even took particular pains over my appearance. But I *was* strapping. Any fool could say that for me. Here I was, barely fifteen, and I already towered over my aunt and uncle and my cousins and schoolmates—and Miss Rogers, too, of course. She wasn't hardly knee-high to a grasshopper anyhow. But I liked her just fine.

So it was a sorry day when we closed in on the end of another school year. Miss Rogers asked me to stay after to help her tidy up. I picked up the broom as usual, and started in on the floor.

"Simon?"

"Yes, ma'am?"

"You may put down the broom. I really wanted to have a private talk with you."

"Ma'am?"

She pointed to a spot on the bench facing her desk. I sat, hanging on to the broom. Wasn't sure where to leave it, with the sweeping still undone.

"Simon," she began again. "Simon . . ."

I grinned. "You've got my name down pat, Miss Rogers."

She sighed. "I do, indeed. As well I might." A frown formed around the edges of her mouth. She toyed with some of that golden hair of hers. "Simon," she tried again. "This is very hard for me to say, but you realize . . ."

"Yes, ma'am?"

"You realize you've just completed third grade. For the fourth time."

"Yes, ma'am. It was more of a pleasure than usual."

Her brow started in knitting. "Be that as it may." Then she took a deep breath and finally let it out. "I believe you've plumbed the depths of third grade, Simon. I believe it's time for you to move on."

I perked up. "That mean I'm finally promoted to fourth?"

"Unfortunately, no. You're already my oldest student, Simon Green. As much as I've enjoyed your companionship, it's time for you to brave the world. To spread your wings."

"You're kicking me out, Miss Rogers?"

"I'm graduating you, Simon. There's a difference."

I scratched my head. It was a fine, full thatch of hair. Not soft and golden, like Miss Rogers's, though. More like hay at harvesting time. I scratched some more. I hadn't figured on being graduated for another few years, easy. If third grade had taken this long, only consider the challenges of fourth and fifth. That didn't even take into account *sixth*, which is what the school went up to.

"I will miss you, Simon. I'll miss your help chopping wood for the stove. And your cleaning and fixing everything in sight. And you're so *good* with the little ones—"

"What do I do next?" I broke in. "Uncle Lucas and Aunt Maybelle, well, they're happiest when I'm off to school."

"Can't you help on the farm?"

I shrugged. "My cousins, they don't take to my messing about with their inheritance." I brightened. "But they do say as how I'm a fine mucker! Think there's a future in manure, Miss Rogers?"

She shook her head. Sadly, I thought. "Not everyone appreciates your finer talents, Simon. But I'm certain . . ." She rose from behind her desk. "I'm certain there's a place for you in this world. Just think about what you like best, Simon. Think about it, and I'm sure you'll find a solution."

"Thank you, Miss Rogers." I guessed I was dismissed. I set down the broom for the last time and took off for home.

The entire three-mile tramp back I cogitated over Miss Rogers's words. One phrase kept coming back to me. *It's time to spread your wings . . . Spread your wings.*

A hawk swooped over my head and I followed its flight. Right over the neighbor's turkey farm. My pea-sized brain lit on that flock of dumb turkeys. I walked closer and they stared at me, gobbling.

"Hey, Simon."

I glanced up. "Hey, Mr. Buffey. Your birds are looking fine."

"Looks could kill." He started in grumbling right off. Everyone knew Mr. Buffey was the biggest grumbler in Missouri. "They swelled this year when I wasn't watching. Size of the flock just tripled."

"That's fine luck," I offered.

"Not if you ain't got the market." He pulled out a wad of tobacco and bit off a chaw. "Here I got all these eating turkeys—eating me out of house and home."

"You can't sell 'em off in St. Louis?"

"That's a fifty-mile walk," Mr. Buffey kept on griping. "And they got turkeys enough."

"Seems to me, Mr. Buffey, seems to me . . ."

"What do it seem to you, Simon?" He spit out a stream of tobacco juice. Them dumb turkeys around him went scrabbling after it.

"Seems to me if they don't need turkeys here in Missouri, you ought to take 'em where they are wanted."

He humphed. "Sure and certain. I got me all summer to walk a thousand turkeys out West, where they's wanted."

I scratched my head again. "How far out West, Mr. Buffey?"

"Why, someplace like to Denver! I was just readin' in the papers about Denver. Biggest boomtown you ever saw, what with gold littering the very streets like it is. But they ain't got nothin' to eat there but beans and bread and coffee, three times the day. Turkeys on the hoof'd go for five dollars a head out there."

"What'd they go for hereabouts?"

"Two bits." He spat once more in disgust.

I stared at the turkeys again. "I ain't got nothing to do all summer, Mr. Buffey."

"What's that?"

"I said, ain't a solitary thing holding me down. I could walk your turkeys to Denver, Mr. Buffey."

"*You*, Simon?" He laughed. "*You* walk my turkeys to Denver? Near a thousand miles?" He laughed some more as if I'd just made his day.

Well, a few insulting words were one thing. Didn't like it when people outright laughed at me, though. I set off for the last mile down the road to home, without a single, civil farewell.

Only now, spreading my wings somehow kept coming back to turkeys.

I forked three big pork chops onto my plate at dinner that night. "Pass the potatoes, Cousin Ned." A mountain of mashed potatoes joined my chops. I drowned it all in thick gravy. Shoveled in a bite.

"Uncle Lucas?"

"Eh? Can't hear you for the mashies, Simon."

I swallowed and waited on my next bite, famished though I was. "Know that old wagon falling apart behind the barn?"

"What of it?"

"If I was to fix it up, could I have it?"

Uncle Lucas grunted. Cousins Ned, Homer, Pete, and Marcus stared at me over their own heaping plates with their beady little eyes. They was probably figuring on what part of their inheritance that old broken-down wagon was. Aunt Maybelle, at the bottom of the table, took an interest, too.

"What you want with that old wreck, Simon?" she asked.

I shoveled in another bite, considering. Finally spit out the news. "Got me graduated from school today. Fixing on setting up in business."

Their blank looks turned devious. Each and every one of 'em.

"On my own," I added. I sank my teeth into a chop to let them digest that.

Aunt Maybelle dabbed her apron at a corner of her eye. "You'll be leaving us, Simon? After all these years?"

"God willing, Aunt Maybelle."

Uncle Lucas downed a draft of his cider. "Supposin' you was to fix that old wagon." He stopped. "Supposin' I was to give it to you. Out of the kindness of my heart, as a sort of inheritance. In memory of my dear sister Samantha—God rest her soul—departed these ten long years—"

"Sure as shooting not in memory of her good-for-nothing husband, Samson, departed—but not to his just rewards—these same ten long years!"

Aunt Maybelle just had to tack that on. She'd done so with regularity over those aforementioned years.

Always made me wonder about the pa I couldn't hardly remember. I laid down a bare bone and set to with another chop.

"Just supposin' . . ." Uncle Lucas peered at me. "What you figure pullin' it with?"

"Mules," I answered promptly. "My four mules that I hand-fed from foals, when their mamas give up on them."

Well, that started a row.

"Pa!" yelled Cousin Homer. "Since when's those mules Simon's?"

"Just 'cause he raised 'em hisself?" Ned added.

"And trained 'em," Marcus throwed in.

"Just 'cause they won't do a durned thing for nobody else!" Pete whined.

I cleared off the last of my potatoes and gravy and reached for the platter of chops. "I'll pay you for 'em."

Stunned silence.

"Also pay you for the full load of shelled corn I'll be needing."

"Why, Simon Green, you ain't got a plugged nickel to your name," Aunt Maybelle finally choked out.

"Don't now. Will by the end of summer."

"You expect me to let you have them mules and corn on speculation, Simon?" Uncle Lucas's piggy eyes spread as wide as they ever got.

I laid three more chops on my plate and dribbled the gravy nice and slow. "Yep. If you want to be rid of me for good and final."

The cousins started in nudging each other around me. Ned finally spoke up.

"Write out a contract, Pa. Make him sign it, nice and legal." Ned snickered. "He does know how to sign his name. Should, after four years in the third grade!" The snicker grew into a guffaw. Ned finally settled some. "Put down about how that there wagon is Simon's complete and full inheritance. And write down the price of the corn and mules, too. Going rates."

Aunt Maybelle got up from table. "How about some pie? In honor of our Simon's new business."

Nary a one of 'em asked me what that business might be.

Out in the backyard after supper, I stripped to my trousers and doused a bucket of water over my head and shoulders. Put on my clean Sunday shirt and slicked down my hair. Cousin Pete spied my efforts.

"Simon's got a sweetheart! Simon's got a sweetheart!"

I didn't deign to make an answer, just mounted my lead mule, Sparky, bareback, and took off down the road to Union. Sooner than later I got to the schoolhouse and knocked on the door back behind. That's where Miss Rogers lived. She opened the door, a surprised look on her face.

"Why, Simon!"

"Evening, ma'am." I shuffled from one big foot to

the other for a moment or two. All the time she kept on staring at me.

"You're all spruced up, Simon. What's the occasion?"

"Wondered if I might have a word, ma'am."

"That would be a rare pleasure. Even if we only parted this afternoon." She stood aside and waved me into her little room.

I hadn't ever been there before. Not in all these years of schooling. It was her private territory. Most creatures have one. Mine was beneath that same old wagon I'd just saved from rotting to death. Many's the summer's night I lay underneath its bed, just content to be away from the house and my cousins. Staring at the stars through the gaps in its slats, wondering if my mama was up there somewheres keeping an eye on me. Now I spun around slowly, taking in Miss Rogers's territory.

"I suspicioned it'd be nice. Like you."

She smiled. "Do take a seat, Simon. I'll fix us a cup of tea."

There were only two chairs by the tiny table in a corner. I took one of them. Then I tried to figure on what to do with my long legs. They never seemed to get in the way like this in the schoolroom next door.

A china cup was set in front of me. On a saucer. There was painted rosebuds all over both. The handle on that cup looked to break in pieces if I was to even touch it with my thick fingers. A matching teapot finally joined it all atop the lace tablecloth. Miss Rogers sat herself down across from me. She arranged her skirts.

"We'll just let the tea steep a moment, Simon."

"Yes, ma'am."

We waited, both staring at that teapot. Miss Rogers finally reached for it and poured for the both of us.

"There now." She smiled again. "You may begin, Simon. Tea does help to settle nerves, I've found."

I made for the cup and managed not to disgrace myself. That tea was soothing. The cup skittered back into its saucer. I took a deep breath.

"It's about spreading my wings, ma'am. I've made a start on it."

One eyebrow rose. "Already?"

"Yes, ma'am. I've lined up the wagon and the mules and the corn. That leaves but the turkeys."

"Turkeys?" She set down her own cup. "Turkeys."

"Yes, ma'am. Mr. Buffey's got a thousand to spare, and I can have them for a quarter apiece . . ." Then I set my elbows on the table and started explaining. About Denver. And the turkey walk.

Miss Rogers listened all the way through. She really listened. By the time I got to the end, both eyebrows had lifted clear up her forehead. She raised a hand and smoothed them back down again. "That is an amazing story, Simon."

"Ain't a story," I protested. "It's pure fact." I edged

13

my elbows off the table. "And I know birds. I'm comfortable with them. It's something I can do, Miss Rogers!"

"Well." She remembered to pick up her cup again. "I do believe you could! How can I help?"

I knew exactly how she could help. That's why I'd come. "First off, my multiplication weren't ever too strong. But the numbers are nice and round. Wanted you to check them for me."

I pulled out a scrap of paper. "See here? One thousand turkeys times twenty-five cents." I glanced across to her. "Seems to me that'd make two hundred and fifty dollars."

Miss Rogers, she didn't even need to glance at my scrap. She just beamed. "You remembered about adding the zeros. And even moving the decimal point. I'm so proud of you, Simon!"

"Thank you, ma'am." That decimal point had given me a few bad moments. But now came the really hard part. I tried to figure on what to do with my hands, since they seemed to get in the way of conversing. I finally sat on them.

"That just leaves me with finding two hundred and fifty dollars to buy Mr. Buffey's flock. What I need is a partner, Miss Rogers. Come Denver, that partner's money would increase. Like loaves and fishes."

Miss Rogers's eyebrows, they rose some more. Sky-high.

Sparky and me, we trotted back home that night in clouds of glory. Miss Rogers had said it was the most interesting business proposition she'd ever heard. Especially coming from someone generally considered pea-brained. We had an appointment to meet at the town bank in the morning. Miss Rogers was going to invest her life savings from teaching in my turkey walk. Course, that meant I had to succeed. The saddest thing I could think of was having Miss Rogers lose her life savings.

Back at the farm, I unbridled Sparky and gave him a rub. Then I stroked the fine velvet on his long ears.

"You and me are going to have ourselves a time," I murmured to him. "You and me and your brothers. We're going to have a good, long walk. We're going to see the world. And we're going to make something of ourselves."

After Sparky brayed his approval, I grabbed a saddle blanket and spread it under my wagon. Instead of counting the stars, I lay there figuring on how to fix it up strong. Really strong.

❦ TWO ❧

That wagon was nearly good as new before another thought hit me. About something I'd forgotten. It was a week or so later.

In the meantime, I'd been to see Mr. Buffey and arranged to buy up his turkeys. Considering as how I was doing the man a favor, getting all them hungry birds off his back, he didn't make it easy on me. Oh, he'd stopped laughing right enough as soon as he laid his peepers on the color of my money. But then he set in to scheming.

"You want the pleasure of destroying my birds, Simon Green, it's all right by me." He eyed the bills in my hand again. "But these ain't your usual whites. These is *bronze* turkeys, worth a good deal more than what you be offering."

Well, I knew they was *bronze* turkeys all along. Wasn't color-blind, was I? That's another reason I took to Mr. Buffey's flock from the start. His birds shimmered in the sunlight. With that touch of green, they was the closest things to peacocks in these parts. Also, I knew for a fact they was better-natured than whites. Had much calmer dispositions. They'd be a sight easier to walk.

"Won't do no good trying to up the price on me, Mr. Buffey." Which is what he was trying to do. I caught the signs right enough. Hadn't I watched Uncle Lucas haggle for years? "Underneath the feathers, turkeys is turkeys. And I'm offering top market value, fair and square. The same figure you give me not three days past."

He spit in frustration. "Didn't know we was bargaining three days past, did I?"

"Take it or leave it, Mr. Buffey." That's also what Uncle Lucas would say next, turning away a little, like he hardly cared. I followed suit. "There be a few other flocks in these parts. Might just have a look at them."

The man struggled mightily, then his hand reached out to snatch the money.

I pulled it back. "Not yet, Mr. Buffey. When I'm set to go, you'll get your money."

"You want these birds, you take 'em off my hands now. *You* feed 'em till you're set to go!"

"You find another buyer betwixt times, Mr. Buffey, *you* sell them for a better price."

He spit again and shoved his twitching fingers into a pocket. He knew the same as me there wasn't any other buyer to be found.

So I had my birds. But that other thought that'd been bothering me came again. It came so strong I missed a hammer blow and half mashed my thumb. I stuck it in my mouth and sucked. *Somebody* had to drive the feed wagon. But *somebody* had to herd the turkeys, too. And wasn't no way I could be two places at the self-same time.

"Son of a gun. I'm gonna need me a drover."

I set down the hammer and headed straight to town on Sparky. There I learned as how word of my doings had been getting around. Wasn't much else transpiring in our piece of Missouri, so it only made sense. I knew how fast it'd spread when the townsfolk saw me coming and started in nudging each other, the way my cousins tended to. A few of the older fellows what'd been to school with me and graduated long since commenced the torture.

"Well, hey. Looky see!"

"It's Simple Simon, the turkey boy!"

"Simon Green, long and lean, nothing in his head but birds and beans!"

Ignoring the lot of them, I continued past the county courthouse to swing off Sparky in front of the general store. The usual layabouts were lounging in front, whittling and spitting.

"Morning," I offered.

I got a few grunts for my efforts. I tried again.

"Morning. I'm looking for a mule skinner. Know of anybody that'd be needing work?"

Charley Kent set down his whittling knife to poke at Ed Heller. "What you say, Ed? Boy asked a civil question. Who do we know can skin mules?"

Ed Heller cackled. "Funny you should ask, since the top mule skinner in these parts ain't but a stone's throw away from us. Know anybody else what's been on the Santa Fe Trail?"

Charley Kent cackled right back. "You referrin' to Bidwell Peece?"

"Who else might I be referrin' to, Charley?"

I cleared my throat. "Mighty kind of you to come up with a name, gentlemen. Any idea where I might find this Mr. Peece?"

A sudden ruckus from behind me broke the morning's tranquillity. I turned to watch the sorriest specimen of humanity I'd ever seen being propelled through the saloon doors. Right off the board walk and into the dust of the street.

Charley and Ed pointed and roared.

The man lay there in a jumble of loose arms and legs. The next minute, another projectile came through the same swinging doors. This one was yelping. Naturally, I went over to give them both a hand. Looked as if they needed it. I started with the man.

"Mr. Peece?"

"Wha . . . ?"

19

Red-rimmed eyes stared at me. I hefted him upright. Dusted him down. "Mr. Bidwell Peece?"

He ran calloused hands through his thinning gray hair. "In person. Last I noticed." He staggered back against the saloon walk. "What can I do for you, boy?"

"It's work I've got for you, sir," I answered. "Work, and maybe a little adventure. If you'd honor me by considering it."

With effort, Mr. Peece stood a little taller. He still was a mighty smallish sort of man. But there looked to be some wire beneath the skin. Just needed to be tensed into shape again.

"Consider anything," he mumbled. "If you was to buy me a drink first."

I steered him from the saloon solicitously. "Strong drink weakens a man, Mr. Peece, sir. You come along with me and we'll have us a nice talk."

Somehow I managed to get him atop Sparky. I led him back to the farm. The second critter turned out to be a small, short-haired, black-and-white dog. He trailed behind us, tail between his legs.

It took three days to dry out Mr. Peece. I set him in the bed of my wagon and just kept working around him. Course, I had to tie him up to keep him there. Gag him, too, when he got to ranting and raving. Aunt Maybelle wouldn't have approved of the noise or the man.

Once each day I loosed the bonds and carried him down to the cow pond and threw him in for a dip. On the third day he came out spluttering. And mad as a wet hen.

"What in tarnation's going on! Who the devil are you?"

So then we had to have introductions all over again. His eyes weren't red anymore. Fact of the matter is, they turned out a real sharp blue. Sober, Mr. Bidwell Peece weren't no man's fool. He was still weak as a kitten, though. I snuck some food from the kitchen to feed him up. Then we really talked.

First thing he asked after was Emmett.

"Who's Emmett?"

"My little black-and-white dog. Seen him around?" I gave a whistle. Emmett trotted up.

Well, you never seen anything like the look on that dog's face when he saw his master in his right mind again. Sheer happiness. His tail set in to wagging at last. Course, Mr. Peece, he lit up like he'd died and gone to his reward, too. They fooled around some and then we got back down to business. Turkey and Denver business. When I finished my story, Mr. Peece wiped his face from all those doggy kisses and walked over to Sparky and Snowball standing in their corral. Straight off he checked their teeth.

"These is fine mules you got here, Simon."

"Appreciate it. Raised 'em myself."

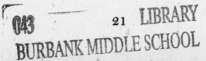

He moved on to Brown Boy and Rocky. "Young and strong. Got lots of pull in 'em."

"I was figuring on that."

"Plenty enough pull for the eight hundred miles or so to Denver, seems to me." He was still stretched over the railing. "With the right skinner, of course."

"Course."

He ran a hand down the nearest flank. My mules weren't skittish with him at all. Not the way they was with Uncle Lucas and the cousins.

"Such fine animals deserve the best."

"My way of thinking percisely, Mr. Peece."

"Might be time to move on anyhow," he muttered to himself. Then he turned to me. "What you offering as pay, boy?"

"To the right man?"

"To the right man."

I considered, even though I'd been considering the subject for the entire three days I'd been ministering to Mr. Peece. Finally I spoke up.

"I'd want my skinner to love my mules first. I'd want him to treat 'em right. On account of they're better than most human beings."

He nodded. "Agreed. On all counts."

"Next, I'd want my skinner to have an interest in the enterprise. Seems to me if he had an interest—a deep interest—in getting there safe and sound . . ." I caught his eyes. "Not only him, but all of us, me and the birds, too . . ."

Mr. Peece nodded again.

"Well, then, for such a person, it seemed to me that a working partnership might prove useful."

"What kind of partnership, boy?"

"A *percentage* kind of partnership." Miss Rogers had been giving me a little extra tutoring this last week. Business-type tutoring at night, so's I wouldn't get gulled come Denver. "A percentage instead of wages. Fact of the matter is, I had in mind five percent of the birds' selling price."

I waited for his response. He was obviously calculating it in his head, already knowing what the birds were worth in Denver. I hadn't minded telling him. The whole rest of the county knew it, too. They just never figured I'd make it to Denver to pick up my money.

Bidwell Peece did a little more counting on his fingers, then looked up at last.

"That's a couple years' pay for a couple months' work . . . Then you have to figure on you puttin' up the capital, and coming up with the idea to begin with . . ." He shook his head. "Then again, I get me that far West, what's to keep me from starting a new life?" He paused. "And I ain't never been greedy, but a little more money'd help out with that."

"True." I studied the man again, and decided.

"You keep shaping up, Mr. Peece, we might just talk about ten percent come Denver." I stopped. "Might just."

He held out his hand. "You got you a deal, son."

We shook on it. Emmett came over and rubbed against my leg. First time, even though I'd been feeding him for three days.

I got my wagon brim full up with shelled corn. Mr. Peece and I rigged a covering over the corn so's it wouldn't all scatter come the first bad piece of road. We rigged a roof over the whole thing, too. There was just enough space between the corn and the roof tarpaulin to stow our bedrolls and a few pots and vittles. There'd be enough to shelter come bad weather, too. All that was left was the leaving in the morning.

"Nine hundred and ninety-eight, nine hundred and ninety-nine, one thousand. There." Mr. Buffey started swinging his wooden gate shut against the last of his flock still swarming behind him.

"Hold up, Mr. Buffey." I shoved my hand out to stop the gate. "I only counted nine hundred and ninety-five. You owe me five more birds."

"No such thing, Simon Green!" He put his weight to his side of the gate. "Ain't my fault if you can't count!"

Bidwell Peece added his wiry strength to my own against our side. "You're both off. By ten entire birds. *I* counted nine hundred and ninety!"

Mr. Buffey started seeing red. "Now look here! I

ain't a-goin' to be flamoozled by any half-wit and town drunk! I ain't—"

"One moment, please, gentlemen." Miss Rogers stepped into the fray. She'd come to see me off, and her lifetime savings, too. My, but she looked fresh and fetching in her sky-blue summer frock and bonnet. She smiled at all of us. "In point of fact, *my* count was nine hundred and eighty-five. I believe you owe Simon another fifteen birds, Mr. Buffey."

The crowd behind Miss Rogers set in to chuckling. Half the district had turned out for the event this morning. And each and every one of them had a different tally on my birds. But being as Miss Rogers was the only schoolteacher amongst them, they stood up for her expertise, even if they didn't know it was her money behind me. Nobody knew but the two of us—and the town of Union's bank president. We thought we'd leave it that way.

"Give 'im his full count, Buffey!"

"It needs to be a fair shake!"

Why the crowd had taken such interest had nothing to do with me personal. It had more to do with this being the biggest event in Franklin County since the free-soil troubles between Missouri and bleeding Kansas a few years back. Then the farmers was betting on how many people John Brown would massacre over to Kansas Territory. Now they was betting on how many turkeys I'd be getting to Denver. Even

Miss Rogers had allowed as how it was, on the whole, a more salutary occupation of their minds.

Mr. Buffey eased up on his side of the gate. "Trying to bankrupt me. The lot of you."

But I got my fifteen birds still due.

So there I stood in the middle of the dirt road surrounded by one thousand turkeys. Guaranteed by Miss Rogers herself. I counted out the two hundred and fifty dollars a final time and handed it over to Mr. Buffey. He grabbed at it, counted it all over again, then stomped off in the direction of his barn. Not even a thank you very kindly.

"Nice doing business with you, Mr. Buffey," I sang out.

The crowd laughed and spread out from my flock. The turkeys, they just stood there, staring at the new sights, gobbling with as much interest as they were able. Mr. Peece pulled himself up the wagon seat and picked up the reins.

"You about ready, son?"

I took a final glance around. Aunt Maybelle and Uncle Lucas and the cousins were at the edge of the throng. I nodded to them.

"See you don't forget that mule money, Simon," Cousin Ned called over.

"And the feed money," Uncle Lucas added.

"You got our address writ down the way I said?" Aunt Maybelle asked. "So's you can send it to us first thing?"

So much for ten years of my life. All they'd be missing was the money due. I nodded again. They was already heading off to their own wagon, shaking their heads. The other farmers were drifting away, too. That left Miss Rogers. Suddenly I felt a little pang of something. Deep down inside. Didn't mind seeing the backs of the rest of 'em, but Miss Rogers . . .

"Ma'am?"

"Simon dear."

She came right over and gave me a hug. It was a proper hug. She sure did smell clean and good.

"I'm relying on you, Simon," she murmured. "And I'm trusting you every step of the way. Praying for you, too, just for good measure."

"Thank you, ma'am."

Miss Rogers stood back to look me over a final time. She studied me long and hard, not even noticing one of my turkeys pecking at her kidskin boots. I gave it a gentle shove with my foot.

"You're really growing up, Simon. Truly spreading your wings. Don't you ever let anybody make fun of you or your enterprise on this trip. They'll only be saying things from jealousy, because you're doing something, and they're not. You're going to make a fine job of it, going to be a fine man one day."

She pressed something into my hand.

"Here. Save this for grave emergencies. And for sending me a message when you arrive." Her eyes twinkled. "You send me an exact count of how many birds you walk all the way to Denver, Simon. Understand?"

"Yes, ma'am, Miss Rogers. I understand fine."

I pocketed the money. Then I bent down to Emmett, waiting patiently at my feet. I rubbed behind his ears, where he liked to be rubbed. I whispered into the closest ear.

"All right, now, Emmett. Never you mind that these birds are all bigger than you. You're smarter, and you're in charge of the left flank. I'll take on the right. Just like we practiced with them chickens back at the farm."

Emmett yipped with excitement.

"I'm ready, Mr. Peece," I hollered when I straightened up again. "Emmett and the birds, they're ready, too."

Mr. Peece let out a whoop and we commenced the great turkey walk.

☙ THREE ☙

It was a perfect June day. Fields of corn was green and growing to the right and left of the road West. My turkeys sure looked fine plowing down the center of that road, their feathers gleaming in the sun. My, but they went at a clip once they got the feel of freedom beneath their feet. That first day we must have made twenty-five miles.

Mr. Peece, he kept the mules going to the front of us, and the turkeys followed like he was the Pied Piper himself. Emmett, he thought he'd died and gone to heaven, he was that happy having tails to nip at and a flock to keep organized. And even better than all that, when we fixed to camp, we didn't need to dig into our supply of corn. Those birds just mowed down the surrounding grass before tucking up for the night.

I started a cook fire, then lounged next to it while Mr. Peece flung some bacon slabs in the pan.

"What kind of a dog is Emmett, Mr. Peece?" I finally wondered aloud.

"Well, now, he's a terrier. Terriers usually love to hunt. After today, though, seems to me he's got him a little sheepdog somewhere."

"More'n a little." I smoothed the short hair of the dog splayed out on my lap. "I think Emmett's found his true calling."

Come first light, I didn't have to do a thing with those turkeys. They was already gliding down from the trees they'd taken roost in, scrabbling about, some of 'em even heading off to the West. Never saw birds so keen to travel.

Course, then, Mr. Peece and I, we had to swallow our coffee and breakfast bacon right fast. Emmett was having a time keeping the birds from getting to Denver before we did.

Things went along fairly fine all morning. We walked through the hamlet of Adamsburg, pretty much hogging the road. People saw us coming, they shook their heads in amazement. Carts and wagons, they tended more to see those huge, striving turkeys as hordes of locusts. They pulled to the side of the dirt road and give us plenty of leeway.

It wasn't till we hit the town of Mount Sterling that we come up against something I hadn't given much thought to. Course, there was a lot of things in this life I hadn't given much thought to. Rivers was high up on that list.

I'd set eyes on the Missouri River a few times. That was on account of the fact that it wasn't but a few miles to the north of Uncle Lucas's farm, and Union, the town my school was in, where I'd found Bidwell Peece. I had talked some with Miss Rogers over the general plan of the trip, though. We'd decided to steer clear of the big river and stay with the road, far as it went. This was mostly because the railroad ran along the river.

Now, I had a certain amount of faith in my birds, but I knew for a fact they wouldn't take to no railroad. My flock hadn't been too flighty yet, but set them next to a steaming, bellowing locomotive, and Hades only knew what mischief they'd get up to.

Well, there wasn't any railroad in Mount Sterling. There was, however, the Gasconade River. Just like that. Moving due north to meet up with the Missouri. Blocking our way West.

Mr. Peece, he pulled the wagon to a halt just above the ferry landing. The ferryboat was loading up to go across. Mr. Peece looked back at me and the birds.

"How we gonna get them turkeys on that little ferryboat, Simon? Take about thirty trips to pass 'em across." He pulled off his slouch hat to swipe at his forehead. "Then there's the toll to consider. Toll on a thousand birds'd almost wipe us out complete."

I took in the sight with some trepidation. It weren't a *huge* river, like to the Missouri, but that Gasconade

31

was sure and certain too deep and fast to wade across. Meanwhile, my birds were flocking up around me, excited like, crowding near the banks of the water, gobbling and clicking their silly heads off. Emmett was standing stock-still, not sure what was required of him. Behind us all, a few dozen of the townsfolk were starting to take an interest in our situation.

"*Hoo!* Where the durn fools think they's a-goin'?"

"*Haw!* Goin' to drown them birds and put 'em out of their misery."

"Whyn't we save 'em the trouble? I could fancy me a turkey supper tonight! How about you, George?"

"Now that you mentions it, Elmer, I could, too. Easy."

I considered the men closing in on us. Then I twisted around to study the river again. I wasn't brought up to quick thought, but quick thought was needed at that moment . . . What happened to birds that was riled good and proper?

I knew the answer to that one. But could my turkeys be counted on to perform what came natural to them? I bent down to Emmett. His pointy little ears were already cocked, waiting for orders.

"Go get 'em, boy! Chase those turkeys straight into the river!"

Emmett gave me an odd look for an instant, but I stood firm. Then I rounded to one side of the flock and let out a godawful rumpus. Emmett took off to the other side, the way we'd been doing for a day and a half. This time, though, he set in to barking up a storm. Together, we drove our birds to the very brink of the Gasconade River. Then we drove them into it.

Except they didn't go into the river. Instead, they spread their wings and flew. Straight and clear. All the way across that water. I held my breath, amazed at the wonder of it. Those bronze feathers surely did look a beautiful sight swooping so graceful through the sky. When the turkeys came to the other side, I was still holding my breath.

Would they just keep on flying? Away from me forever? I could see Miss Rogers's lifetime savings floating off to the great beyond. To some turkey Zion in the sky.

My breath returned when they set themselves down again. Nice as you please. And there they stood. That entire flock was waiting on me to the other side of the river. They even raised their heads—after they'd settled their wings again—raised their heads and peered back across, like to say, "What are you waiting on, Simon? *We're* here."

I swung toward Bidwell Peece. He'd gone pale as a ghost under his sunburn. Slowly he clapped the hat back atop his sparse hair and jostled the reins still gripped in one hand. Sparky and Snowball led the mule team down the riverbank and onto the waiting ferryboat. Emmett and me followed. As the boat was casting off, I looked back up at the townsfolk. They were in a clump, sort of shambling from one foot to the other, still too disbelieving to say aught.

"A turkey supper'll cost you five dollars the bird," I shouted back to them. "But you'll have to come to Denver to get it!"

Those birds must have been more tuckered out from their exertions than they looked. We hadn't made more than a mile or two after the river when we passed through a nice stand of hickory and black walnut. Without a by-your-leave, my turkeys took to the trees, roosting for the night. All it needed was for one of them to have the idea. Pretty soon the entire thousand birds was settled in, reddish-purple heads poked under their wings.

It happened so fast, I had to yell Mr. Peece and the wagon back. He swiveled his neck from the mules, then his eyes went wide.

"Where the dickens's them birds?"

I pointed up to the trees.

His bony Adam's apple stretched up, with his neck, as he verified what he couldn't believe. "But it's hardly three of the afternoon!"

"*You* want to get 'em back down?"

"No." He slumped down from the wagon seat. "But I *would* like a drink. Don't think all this drama is good for my heart."

I handed him the water jug.

He shoved it aside. "Weren't the sort of drink I had me in mind of."

I took a swig. "Only kind of drink you'll be seeing till Denver—if that ten percent still interests you."

Mr. Peece stared longingly down the road we'd just traveled. "It's only a couple of miles back to town. I'd be here in camp afore nightfall."

I drank again. "By nightfall I'd have me another drover."

He nodded. "The way you do things, you probably would, at that." He pulled himself together and brightened some. "Seeing as how we're stuck here for the duration, I might as well take the opportunity to whip up one of my culinary delights."

I spit out a mouthful of water. "What in thunder's a *culinary delight*?"

"Gather some kindling, Simon. Lots of kindling. You're about to learn some new tricks."

By sundown, the smell of Mr. Peece's culinary delight must have been wafting through three counties. Least enough so that we picked up a stray to join us for supper.

In point of fact, I hadn't helped much in creating that supper, aside from gathering firewood. After I'd got a good pile growing near the wagon, I took off back to the woods to where this stream we'd been following wandered. Then I pulled off my boots and woolen socks and sank my toes into the water. It felt just fine after all the miles I'd put beneath these feet the last two days. More miles than I'd ever gone in my entire life, seemed like. Next thing you know, I was sleeping like a baby.

Least, I must have drifted off, 'cause when I come to again, darkness had started settling down through the leaves over my head. I propped myself up on one elbow and yawned. Then I jumped.

"Who's there?" Seemed like a face was staring at me from across the stream. A dark face.

"Nobody."

I sat up. "*Nobody* can't talk, can he? I mean, it stands to reason. If nobody is truly not there, then—"

The face came closer, followed by a body that splashed through the stream. "I gives up. I gives myself up to you, master. You looks harmless enough. Just feed me! I'm that hungry—"

"Whoa, now." I straightened my back. "I ain't nobody's master, and never mean to be. Even Uncle Lucas never kept no slaves." I stopped to consider. "Then again, maybe he figured he had enough between me and Aunt Maybelle and the cousins—"

"Don't know what you's goin' on about, but I'm *hungry*, master. That smell come through clear to the other side of the woods, and my nose done led me to you. I'm givin' myself up. You can get the reward. Beyond caring, is what I am. Just feed me!"

I finally remembered about my boots and socks.

"Hold on a minute till I get these on." Then I was up, standing next to a boy about my age. My height, too, if he was to stop bowing and scraping long enough to tell. But even with that, you could see he weren't hardly more than skin and bones next to me.

"Now let's start over again. Without this *master* folderol. I'm Simon Green. Who're you, besides hungry and nobody?"

He finally grinned. "Jabeth Ballou, from down in—"

I held up a hand. "Don't want to know where from. But you hear somebody hollering? That'd be Mr. Peece. I reckon his culinary delight's about ready to eat. And from the size of the pot he was cooking it in, there's bound to be enough for three."

Mr. Peece, he hardly even blinked when he saw me coming out of the woods followed by that truly scrawny black boy.

"Company for supper? Good. Got enough for an army here, and I like my bean pie to be appreciated."

I moved closer to the bubbling cauldron. Aunt Maybelle's old iron pot sure and certain hadn't smelled this good when I liberated it from the back shed where she stowed used-up things. "Bean pie?" I sniffed again.

"Bean and bacon and molasses pie," Mr. Peece expanded. "Invented it myself."

I turned to the company. "Set yourself down, Jabeth, before you collapse. Hope you don't mind eating out of the frypan, 'cause we only got two tin plates to our names."

Jabeth Ballou didn't do no more kowtowing after he'd eaten. He'd stuffed himself too full. He lounged there in the darkness surrounding the fire, groaning blissfully for about fifteen minutes while Mr. Peece and I played with our toothpicks. Then he finally spoke.

"That was a mighty fine crust, Mr. Peece, sir. Flaky on top, juicy underneath. My compliments."

"Thankee," Mr. Peece drawled. "Took some pains with it."

"I knowed it. If my mama was alive, even she couldn't top it."

That sparked my interest some. "You an orphan, Jabeth? Like me?"

"Recent," he said. "Just recent. Which is why I took off." He belched gently and rubbed his distended stomach. "Figured I'd make for the Kansas Territory and freedom."

"Funny thing—" Mr. Peece started.

"—but Kansas Territory is where we're headed," I finished. "Near as far as it goes. Near as far as the Utah Territory."

Jabeth Ballou's black eyes glinted with the firelight. He grinned for the second time since I'd met him.

❦ FOUR ❦

Nobody said anything about Jabeth's status come morning. Or hardly anything. We just got up with the birds and made ready to move on. In point of fact, it was Jabeth who woke us.

"*Ow!*" he yelled. "Help! . . . Heeelp!"

I rolled over in my blankets and cranked open an eye. There was Jabeth just a-lyin' stiff as a corpse on the ground, with a plump tom turkey hovering over him, pecking at his hair with interest.

"Shoo him away, Jabeth," I muttered. "He don't mean no harm. Just never seen hair like yours before."

"What *is* it?"

With a sigh, I propped myself up. "Why, it's a turkey. A *bronze* turkey." I reached for a pebble and lobbed it over. The tom took off.

Jabeth sat up and looked around. "They's all over!" He near to screamed it, freezing up again. "Giant turkeys all over! In the *trees*. On the *ground*. I'm surrounded!"

"Well, I hope to heaven they're all over. And I hope to heaven they keep their weight. Near to thirty pounds, some of them toms. You're looking at my meat and potatoes, Jabeth. My future. These is *my* turkeys."

Jabeth shivered.

That set me to thinking again. "Weren't you brought up on a farm? How is it you've never seen a turkey?"

"Pigs," he said. "The master raised pigs. And a few laying hens. Pigs I could deal with any day. They don't creep up on a body thisaways."

I finally got up to roll my blankets. "You want to trail along with this here business establishment, you got to learn to love turkeys, Jabeth."

He struggled out of the blanket I'd loaned him. "I love turkeys," he said. "I love them to pieces!" But he tiptoed mighty carefully around the fresh batch pecking by his bare feet.

A few hours into our morning exercise, I got to thinking about how Jabeth done steeled himself to run away in the first place. However he could have managed it. That fellow was nothing but a bundle of nervous bones.

Take the way he was walking left flank this very minute. I'd set him to that side so's he could watch Emmett at work and get some training from him. But he didn't seem to be picking up the way of it real fast. What he was doing was flapping his arms ever so often like a scarecrow. Course, with his ragged shirt and pants flapping along with those skinny arms, the overall effect was to upset my birds. I watched him skitter a dozen or so into needless flight. Then I bit the bullet.

"Jabeth?"

"Yes, sir, Mister Simon?"

Least he'd gotten past the *master* part. Still and all. "Just Simon, Jabeth. Simon, plain and pure. I ain't no older than you howsomever I look at it."

"Yes, sir, Simon."

I shut my mouth. He was progressing. And it's not like he'd had all those years Miss Rogers had to learn my name down pat.

"Come walk with me a piece, Jabeth. We'll try us a new tack with your turkey training."

"Yes, sir, Simon." He flapped on over.

We got us to the other side of the town of Linn that day, no thanks to Jabeth Ballou. I watched my turkeys roost themselves in a heavy growth of oak and elm while I pondered over the situation, just standing there, scratching my head.

That fellow had no feeling for birds whatsoever. He was willing, right enough. But he sure and certain wasn't able. Didn't look like a gift he was about to be blessed with, either. I walked over to the wagon where Mr. Peece was ungearing the mules.

"Hey, Simon," he said.

"Hey, Mr. Peece." I tickled Sparky between the ribs. Sparky snorted and gave a little braying laugh.

Mr. Peece tossed down a neck collar. "Your boy don't seem to have an aptitude for birds, Simon."

"That's a fact." I tickled Sparky some more. "I was just worrying over it."

"You could set him off on his own again. He was managing afore he found us."

"Weren't managing. Was starving himself to an early grave, more like."

"Ain't your place to feel responsible, son." Mr. Peece slung off another neck collar.

"Ain't. But I do."

"Then again, he's got a mighty big appetite. And we only provisioned for two."

"I don't begrudge him the food. Just wish I could put a finger on his talent. Miss Rogers always said as how there's a place for every soul in this world. Only needs to be found."

Mr. Peece started in leading Sparky to the stream we'd stopped next to. The turkeys had already availed themselves of it. It might've gone down an inch or two from their thirst, but there was still water enough left.

"Where's Jabeth now?"

I turned back from my considerations of the stream

to Mr. Peece. "Borrowed my knife and took himself off into the woods first thing we stopped."

"Maybe he's figured the situation out for himself, then. Maybe he's already taken off on his own."

"He wouldn't of left for good with my only knife, Mr. Peece. *That* I'm sure of."

Jabeth didn't, neither. He poked out of them woods again about a half hour later. And he came with peace offerings.

"I knowed I didn't do a real fine job for you today, Simon, sir." He handed me a passel of fresh stream trout strung up on some wild grapevine. "But I'll do better tomorrow."

I stared at the fish. Behind me, I could hear Mr. Peece trotting over right fast. "Where'd you get them trout, Jabeth?" he asked.

"In a little crick pool back in them woods."

"How'd you get 'em?" I wondered aloud. "A body can fish thataways, he oughtn't be half-starved to death the way you are."

"Got 'em with your knife, of course." He wiped the blade on an intact square of his trousers and handed it back. "Tied it to a stick and just aimed." He passed the string along to Mr. Peece. "Didn't have no knife when I took off from the master. Never had me one of my own."

I studied the knife in my hand, then slowly pulled

its sheath from my belt. "Here." I handed them both over. "Why don't you just keep on borrowing it for a while. Forget about the turkeys. You're our new provisioner."

"I am?" Jabeth blinked, then made a little dance of pleasure in his bare feet. "I'll just head on back before I lose the light, then. Get us a few more for breakfast. We can keep 'em fresh in that water yonder overnight."

I turned to Mr. Peece, who was already squatting over the catch, cleaning it. He was whistling as he worked. He stopped to grin up at me. "Nothing like a mess of fresh trout to follow last night's bean pie. I do admire fresh trout."

"You reckon he can stay, then?"

"Long as he contributes, son. Long as he contributes." He set to with more gutting. "Speaking of which, whyn't you contribute some of them wild onions growing over the way, Simon? Pan-fried trout is mighty fine stuffed with wild onions."

Jabeth sure did take to my bowie knife. He polished it lovingly after supper, then set in to whittling at a stick he'd fetched back with our breakfast fish. I watched him lazily, thinking about the last whittling I'd seen—back in Union. The whittling on the porch of the general store that had found me Bidwell Peece. Jabeth was whittling different, though, with more of a will.

I watched some more, between fighting to keep my eyes from shutting. It suddenly hit me.

"You making something, Jabeth?"

"What'd you expect?" he fired back.

"Never seen nobody *make* something out of their whittling before."

"What'd you mean?"

"I mean, they just sort of whittles to see them little curls of wood spring up, the longer the curl the better. Then they throws the stick away and starts out fresh on another."

"My mama never taught me to waste time like that. You whittle, you whittles something useful."

I sat up straighter, squinting through the dark. "So what is it you're making, then?"

"Just a minute now, and I'll show you."

Jabeth's long, slim fingers worked that knife like the finest tool. I studied its precision with interest. My bowie knife hadn't ever done that kind of labor before. Finally the blade stopped flashing in the firelight. I glanced over to Mr. Peece to get his opinion. Too late. He was already beginning to snore atop his bedroll. A strange sound jerked my head back. A kind of *haunting* sound.

"Where'd that come from? That sound?"

Jabeth took the stick from his mouth and it stopped. "From my flute."

My jaw dropped open. "You just made you a musical instrument in a few minutes? And you can make it play, too?"

Jabeth flashed a smile. "Get me some solid hunks of wood, can make me a fiddle. I can make that sing, too."

"Son of a gun." I remembered to shut my mouth. "I guess Miss Rogers was correct, as usual."

"Who's Miss Rogers?"

"Only the kindest, loveliest lady in this entire world."

"Like to meet her sometime. Ain't had too much experience with kind, lovely ladies—my mama aside."

Jabeth put that flute to his mouth again. This time the music that came forth sounded just like Miss Rogers. Graceful and twinkling and full of light and life. I lay back onto my own bedroll and shut my eyes. I didn't even bother to explain why Miss Rogers was right, as usual. She just naturally knew how to find the best in any poor soul. I drifted off to sleep, peaceful.

❧ FIVE ❧

Jefferson City was the biggest place I'd ever seen.
People back home had told me it couldn't hold a
candle to St. Louis, but it looked good to me. Take
that Capitol building. Made out of blocks of carved
stone, it was. And it had columns standing all up and
down its front. I couldn't help but stop cold before it
and gape like the farm boy I used to be. Wasn't every
day you got to see the Capitol of the capital city of the
great state of Missouri.

And churches! There was churches any which way
you turned. I counted six or seven of 'em, every reli-
gion you could imagine. But general sightseeing
wasn't why I'd truly come into Jefferson City. Why I'd
truly left our camp just outside of the capital was on
account of a broadsheet that'd been hammered up to
the sign pointing into town. It was the pictures that'd
caught my attention, but I stood and carefully worked
out the words, too, one at a time:

The pictures showed a strange creature with this big old hump just lodging on its back, like it belonged there. Next to it was a lion, and to the other side a tiger. I knew about lions and tigers from a picture book Miss Rogers had in the schoolroom for when she gave her annual talk on deepest, darkest Africa and exotic Asia. I'd heard that talk about eight times over the years. Never thought I'd see me real lions and tigers, though. But here they was, like a gift. Wasn't no way I could turn down that kind of a present. I ran from the broadsheet back to where Bidwell Peece was giving the mules a rubdown.

"I got to go into Jefferson City tonight, Mr. Peece."

His hand stopped its steady stroking motion. "Thought we was just going to head in far enough in the morning to pick up the next road West, seeing as all roads in Missouri spiral into Jefferson City. Thought we was going to avoid confusin' the birds with a real big town."

48

"I ain't taking the turkeys with me, Mr. Peece! I don't want them confused any more than you. But I need to go into Jefferson City. I truly do."

He moved to another section of Brown Boy's flanks and began his rubbing again, a little more tentatively. "I could go with you. Keep you out of trouble."

"What trouble?" Only kind of trouble I could foresee was Mr. Peece getting near any saloons. Of which a genuine river town and capital had to have lots. Even Uncle Lucas had said as how laws ain't never been made on sweet cider.

"Nevertheless, I think it would be a good idea for me to come with you, Simon—"

"Come where?"

Jabeth had finally caught up with us from his day trailing along behind in the woods. This time he had a string of squirrels slung over his shoulder. He offered them to Mr. Peece. "Squirrels was mighty dumb today. Just a-stood there chattering in the trees whilst I let fly with my knife. Hope you knows how to make squirrel stew, Mr. Peece, sir."

That distracted my drover for a moment. His eyes lit up. "Brunswick stew, Jabeth. Simmered with some of that there hard corn we're carrying for the birds. Tastiest thing you ever set your teeth into."

"Fine." I started sauntering off. "You just save me a portion for when I get back."

"Back from where?" Jabeth asked again. "You going

into Jefferson City, Simon, sir? Take me with you, please? I ain't never seen a capital city."

Didn't like to do it, but I had to put my foot down. "Think that's the smartest thing you could do, Jabeth Ballou? If you really and truly have a bounty out on you?"

He hung his head. I turned to Mr. Peece. I could tell saloons had won out over Brunswick stew in his mind again. Could see it in the set of his eyes. I stomped out that temptation fast.

"The two of you got to look after each other and the birds. Now, I'm trusting you both. I won't be that long. Maybe a little past dark, hear?"

The circus was set up on a field next to the river. It was just past a row of big stone and brick houses all squinched up into each other, with long porches running across their fronts on each floor, so a body could set out and admire that Missouri. I admired it for a spell myself. There was one or two flatboats left over from the old days, but mostly it was steamboats pulled up next to the docks. I sure would've liked to see how those paddle wheels worked, but there was no smoke coming from any stacks, so I headed over to the circus tent.

It must have been getting on toward time for the show, because people was starting to line up for tickets. There was lots of youngsters jumping around, excited, and plenty of grownups looking near the same. I didn't buy me a ticket, though, because the only money I had was Miss Rogers's. And that was meant for dire emergencies. So far, I'd only cut into it for that ferryboat toll. I thought maybe I'd find me a hole somewhere in that big tent and see what I could see.

Except there was other things going on along the way to the tent. There was a stand where men were shooting at targets. I walked closer and puzzled out the sign atop it. It said for five cents you could take a chance and win a prize. There was a whole row of prizes just crowding a shelf, too. Over the crack of rifle shots I studied them. *Crockery.* Wasn't nothing but little crockery gimcracks of puppies and kittens and such. I snorted. Didn't look like no nickel's worth of a prize to me.

Farther down the way a little table was set out. Something more interesting was going on there. A fellow in a fancy embroidered vest and garters on his shirt sleeves was giving a pitch about how a sharp person could make his fortune mighty fast. Meanwhile he was playing with these three funny-looking things. Seemed like furry brown balls that'd been sawed in half. They was curious, so I barreled through the crowd of men to see better.

"*Coco-nuts,*" the fellow was chanting. "*Coco-nuts can be faster than the eye, but they don't lie.*"

He lifted one of them coconut things. It was all

hollowed out, and sitting underneath was this shiny silver dollar, nice as you please. Then he clapped that shell back on and swirled the three around some more. Lifted another one. There sat that dollar again.

"Put your money down, gentlemen. It's easy as pie. Coconuts don't lie!"

A fat man next to me offered two bits. Them coconuts started in moving again. When they stopped, he pointed. The shell was lifted. Sure and certain, there was that silver dollar! The fat man picked up his quarter and the dollar both, and walked off looking mighty pleased with himself.

"See how easy it is, gentlemen?" the fellow in the fancy vest said again. He pulled another shiny silver dollar from his vest pocket and slapped it down. "Put your money on the table, make the first piece of your fortune!"

All this time, my fingers were in my pocket, hanging on to Miss Rogers's emergency money. If I was to take a chance on just two bits of it, why, I'd have a lot more back right quick.

I figured for a minute before I could work out exactly how much more that'd be. It finally came to me. Four times as much! Plus I got to keep the original quarter. That way I could buy me a quarter ticket to see the show and be educated by real lions and tigers. Also there was that humpbacked thing I was developing a remarkable interest in. All around, it seemed like an investment even Miss Rogers would be proud of.

I pulled out a quarter and plunked it down. The fellow in the vest grinned up at me.

"Here's a young man with foresight! A young man with big things ahead of him!"

That being the nicest thing anybody'd said to me in some time, I blushed a little.

The gentleman raised all three of them coconuts so's I could see proper that two was empty underneath, and one had the new silver dollar.

"Keep your eye on the coin!"

Then he moved them all around real fast. I stared hard as I could at the one with the money underneath of it. Hard as I could. Finally he stopped. I looked up, a little dizzy.

"Call your choice, young man!"

I looked down again, knowing exactly which one of them coconut things was holding my new silver dollar.

I pointed. He picked up the shell. I stared.

"It ain't there!"

My two bits wasn't, either. It was already in his pocket.

"Gotta keep sharp, young man. Give it another try!"

Well, I *knew* I could do it this time. I fetched out another quarter. Got dizzy again. But this time I didn't lift my eyes. I kept 'em right there on that coconut that held my rightful money. I pointed.

It was empty again.

I raised my head to those grinning eyes. Like a

fox's they was. Now, I ain't ever been known for having a temper, but of a sudden I saw red. I'd just lost me the selfsame thing as two complete turkeys. Didn't help that them other men to the right and left of me was laughing up their sleeves, either.

"You gulled me!"

I reached over that little table for the man in the fancy vest. His face turned shades of green and pink to match the vest stitching as my big hands grabbed ahold of his shoulders and shook.

"You gulled me, and I won't be gulled!"

"It's a game of chance—" he started. He stopped as I shook harder. Then he seemed to gather all his strength together to roar out one word.

"Sam-son!"

The strongest arms I ever felt were pulling me off of the coconut man. I let go of the bundle in my hands to turn and grapple with them. The crowd parted in anticipation of a good old fight. And it would have been, too, if I hadn't of looked up. Past a chest and shoulders every bit as broad and brawny as mine. Into a face near a head taller than me. And clear through eyes as wide and green as my own.

The fight went out of me. I was staring at my own image. Just like when I'd sneak a glance into Aunt Maybelle's looking glass in the parlor back on the farm. Except there was a difference. I knew I was looking at me *older*. He must have been looking at himself *younger*, too, 'cause the strength went out of his grip, the same way. We just stood there, arms dangling by our sides. Just stood and stared at each other.

"What're you doing, Samson?" the man in the vest was shouting. He edged nearer. Cautiously. "That lout near to killed me!"

Samson shoved him away. "Shut up, Cleaver. Ply your gambling tricks on someone else. Not—I *couldn't* be mistaken—on my only son!"

I gulped. It'd taken me a while, as per usual, to come to any conclusions. But how many Samsons could there be in Missouri? How many that was the spitting image of me?

"Pa?" It came out in a squeak. I cleared my throat and tried again. "You my pa, Samson Green, what's been gone these ten long years?"

Those huge arms came around and grabbed me up in a bear hug. Like to take all the stuffing that was left out of me, it did.

"Simon!" Then he said it again. "Simon!"

He dropped me and I worked my lungs like a bellows for a full minute. When I had all my air back, I stared up at him again.

"You're so glad to see me, how is it you didn't come looking back to the farm? How is it you ain't had no other interest in me since Mama went to her reward?"

❦ SIX ❧

I didn't get my answer right then and there. Instead, Pa drug me off by the arm.

"Later. We'll work it all out later. Right now it's time for the show."

He walked me through the big tent opening, right past the crowds pressing to get in. Right past the ticket taker standing there with his hand out. Inside the tent, Pa shoved me into a front-row seat.

"Don't move. I've got to get into my costume."

"What costume?"

"You'll see. Don't dare shift an inch!"

Then he was gone.

I stretched my legs out an inch. Then a full foot. Testing. That tent roof didn't fall in on me. Nothing happened at all. Except the rows of board seats around and behind me started to fill up with people. I settled in to wait.

Pretty soon a man with a big mustache and a black stovepipe hat and red coat came into the center of the tent. Music started sawing up from the three musicians tucked off in a far corner. The circus began.

I near forgot about finding my long-lost pa in the doings of the next hour or so. The show started off with a pretty lady hanging from this little bitty swing right under the tent roof. Swaying to the music, she did some amazing tricks up there. It was kind of hard to concentrate on the tricks, though, on account of the fact that she's wearing next to nothing. I swear. My eyes near to popped out at them delicate legs covered in naught but tight yellow stockings. And the rest of her done up in something shiny—with not a whole lot of that, either. Well, mine wasn't the only eyes popping, I can say that much.

Next come two silly little men dressed up in rags, with big red noses. They fooled around with the swing, too. But it had been lowered barely off the ground, and anyway, they kept tumbling off of it. That got the crowd to roaring. Then there was this trained-dog act that started me thinking about Emmett and how Mr. Peece and Jabeth was doing without me back at camp.

It took them circus people a while, but they finally brought on the lions and tigers. Except there was only one of each. They put 'em in a little cage they built right in the center of the ring, and made them jump through some hoops. The cats didn't take to the work much. Besides which, they was looking a little long in the tooth to begin with.

I guess the humpbacked creatures were the most interesting part of the show. They had three of them. Looked to be a family—a papa, a mama, and a youngster. They was led out and paraded around, all the while the announcer man was explaining as how they were called camels and come from way across the seas in Egypt, the land of the ancient Pharaohs and the Pyramids and the Nile River. He said these animals was remarkable on account of how they could walk through dry deserts for days while carrying heavy burdens, without taking a single drink of water.

I cogitated on that fact while they was paraded around some more. It seemed like a useful talent for a creature to have in a place where there wasn't no water to begin with anyway. Then to prove how strong they was, the circus folks made the papa camel sit down. He complained most bitterly, but folded up his legs and did it. Bundles was piled atop him, and those funny men climbed atop of the bundles. Then they forced the camel to rise up again. He groaned and tottered, but made it all the way around the ring before he was led off for some peace. That's when Pa appeared.

"Ladies and gentlemen," the announcer said. "Next it is my pleasure to present for your amazement and delectation a man as strong as the strongest camel. Stronger even!"

A musician tooted his horn a little. The announcer took off his top hat and waved it.

"Samson—the Strongest Man in the World!"

Out came Pa. He had even less clothes on than that swing lady, only the effect weren't quite the same on him. His bare chest and legs were all greased up. He'd even greased up his thatch of straw-colored hair and slicked it all back from his face. He bowed some, then went to the center of the ring where a bunch of heavy-looking weights had been dragged out onto the sawdust.

Well, Pa proceeded to lift them weights—all of 'em hanging off of bars and marked up in pounds. First the fifty-pound weight, easy as pie. Next the hundred-pound weight. For this he had to bend his knees and flex his big muscles a little. Then he moved on to a hundred and fifty. It started becoming really interesting when he got to the two-hundred-pound weight. Pa, he grunted a lot and made a few strained faces. But he did it.

By the time he's working on the three-hundred-pound bar, that crowd was going wild. They didn't think he could do it. But I knew he could on account of the fact that I've lifted heavier things than that myself. Come rainy season back on the farm, it was *me* Uncle Lucas and the cousins always fetched whenever they'd gone and got a wagon all mired in the mud. Still, Pa made a respectable showing for himself and I cheered along with everyone else.

Finally there was some fancy horses—the announcer called them prize Arabians—prancing around with more near-naked ladies on their backs, and then the circus was over. I leaned back after the crowd had filed out, and waited for Pa.

"Simon?"

My whole body jerked and my eyes flew open. I rubbed them. It had been a long, fairly eventful day.

"Pa? You finished?"

He must have been, because his regular clothes was back on, and he'd rubbed off most of the grease. Except his hair was still slicked back. It made the color much darker.

"For tonight. Let's go somewhere and talk."

"Where?"

"To my cabin on the steamboat."

"You get to travel on a steamboat?"

"The whole circus does. We work up and down the Missouri. The Mississippi, too." He was already striding from the tent, so I took off after him.

Only thing he did while we was walking along the river was to tuck something into my hand. I peered at it in the dark. "What's this?"

"The four bits you lost to Cleaver. I got it back. You need some taking in hand, Simon, if you're dumb enough to get caught by such an old swindle."

"Swindle? You mean them coconuts? But this fat man just before me, he walked off with the dollar easy as—"

He pushed me toward a gangplank. "Get aboard. That fat man was Joe Sellars."

"How'd you know his name?" I stumbled a little on the unfamiliar slant of the planks. "How'd you—"

"He works for the circus, Simon. He ain't nothing but a decoy."

I stopped flat on my feet atop the deck. "A decoy? Like to when a person goes hunting? To fool the ducks? But doing that with people . . . that, that ain't *honest*, Pa!"

Pa grinned through the darkness. "Welcome to the real world, Simon. The smart keep their money, and the suckers get taken. Where you been your entire life, anyhow? No, don't tell me yet. Wait till we get to my cabin."

That cabin was kind of tiny for the two of us, but I managed to sit myself down on one end of the bunk. Pa took the only chair and filled up the rest of the space. Then we started in talking.

"About your mama, son," Pa began. "I want you to know I was struck with grief when she died. Sheer struck." He pulled out a huge handkerchief and ran it past his eyes, then honked into it. "I just took myself away in blind sorrow, knowing I'd never love another woman—"

Somebody knocked at the cabin door. Before either of us could say aught, it opened a crack.

"Samson, darling?" The head of that near-naked lady on the swing popped in. "Ready to take me out for supper, like you promised?"

Pa gulped. "Lila. Something turned up—"

She shoved in farther, pouting all over. "Is that any way to treat your—" Then she spied me. "Who the *devil* is that?"

Well, I blushed from head to foot. First off, here was this lady from the show. True, she'd a few more clothes on now. A skirt, even. But her uppers was still practically . . . I gulped, too. On top of which, she'd already used a word I'd never heard on *any* lady's lips. Why, Miss Rogers would be scandalized clear down to her well-covered ankles!

Pa was shambling up. "Watch it, Lila. This here is my first and only offspring in the flesh."

"First and only?" She giggled.

Pa shoved her back out the door. "Later, Lila. Go practice on your trapeze, or something."

Pa sure liked that word *later*. He plopped back into the chair and turned to me. "Enough of the preliminaries. What brings you to Jefferson City?"

So then I had to tell him the whole story. About being graduated, and leaving the farm, and setting up in business with the turkeys. The entire works.

Pa sat there scratching his head after he'd heard me out. The gesture almost made me start in on my own thatch. I knew right well it weren't an itch but a way of thinking that we both seemed to have.

"You say you paid two bits apiece for these thousand turkeys, Simon?"

"Sure did." He seemed to keep coming back to those birds of mine.

"And they're good for *five dollars* the head come Denver?"

"It's the gospel truth."

He pawed through his hair some more. "Maybe you ain't as dumb as you let on, Simon. At least about the important things."

"Mighty nice of you to consider that, Pa—"

"Still—" He stopped me. "Still and all, there's many a peril between Jefferson City and Denver. You ain't even come to the end of the road yet. You ain't come near to the open prairie, or the mountains, or the wild Injuns. Maybe you need a little more help getting that flock safely through."

"Doing just fine, Pa. Got me top-quality helpers already. Any more'd just get underfoot."

Pa kicked out of his chair and stood up. "A father's place is by the side of his son, Simon. To help him through the trials and tribulations of life. I really think I ought to come along and help out with your little enterprise."

I peered up at Pa. It's not that I mistrusted him exactly. He had saved me from the coconut man. He had gotten my four bits back. Miss Rogers's four bits. He had warned me about some circus folk and their ways. Yet with all that . . .

"How come you're taking such a sudden interest in my welfare, Pa? Seeing that you only just laid eyes on me this very day for the first time in—"

"Ten *years*," he said mournfully.

He pulled out the handkerchief and honked at his nose some more. That nose was different from mine. It had a big bump toward the top, then broadened out a little crookedly. Must have been broken somewhere along the line.

"Ten *long* years. Will I never be forgiven for what sorrow and grief done to me? Will I never be forgiven for abandoning the fruit of my loins at the most tender of ages?" He swooped over me. "Let me make it up to you, Simon. I'm begging you!"

Well, he had my head reeling worse than that coconut man. I didn't know what to do or say. I needed some good advice fast and quick, but Miss Rogers was nowheres near to hand. That only left Bidwell Peece and Jabeth. I shoved myself up.

"Time to be getting back to my camp, Pa. It was right nice bumping into you."

His huge body blocked the door. "You running off on me, son? After what we just shared?"

I stopped when he said *son*. Strange, but it didn't sound the way it did when Mr. Peece called me that—even if I knew for certain sure I wasn't no way connected by blood to my mule skinner. A picture of Bidwell Peece flashed before me. True, he'd been a drunk.

True, he still got tempted by the devil's brew. But his eyes was crisp and blue in that image. And they was offering up real affection for me. I shook my head to clear it.

"Ain't sure I'm your *true* son, Pa. Ain't sure a man can call a boy that unless they's striven and sweated some together."

"That's what I'm trying to do!" Pa protested.

"Ain't sure it can be picked up in the middle of things, either." I reached past him for the doorknob. "Ain't even sure I got me a father at all. But it's something I'll give some thought to."

"But what about—"

I'd managed to get the door partway open. "You're welcome to stop by camp in the morning, Pa. Just to the other side of Jefferson City on the post road from St. Louis. You shake a leg, might still be able to get Miss Lila some supper. She looks to need a little feeding up."

Jabeth was sacked out cold when I made it back to camp. Emmett, too, sprawled atop his chest. Mr. Peece was up, though. Seemed like he'd been pacing around some, because he near to sprung at me when I got into sight of the fire.

"Simon! Are you all right, son? What happened?"

I sat down by the fire while he spooned up a big plate of his Brunswick stew for me. Then I scratched my head. "It's a funny thing, Mr. Peece, but you was dead on right about trouble in Jefferson City."

The ladle stilled in his hand, but he finally got the stew to me. "Tell me about it, Simon. Everything— from the beginning."

⟨ SEVEN ⟩

Thank heaven, my birds decided on making an early morning of it all by themselves. They were down from their roosts and gobbling to go barely after first light.

I shuffled awake, feeling groggy from too little sleep. I rubbed at my cheeks and was surprised by the sudden roughness of them. There wasn't time for to contemplate that, though. Instead, I dropped my hand and squinted through the low-lying mists. Then I gave Jabeth a poke in the ribs.

"Whaah—"

Up popped his head. Atop him, Emmett's pointy little ears went erect.

"We got to get us moving, boys."

"But I don't smell no coffee!"

"Won't be none this morning. Nor breakfast, neither, aside from cold stew. We got to hustle us and the birds down the road."

Jabeth was suddenly so awake, it was as if I'd

dashed him with a pail of water. "Slave catchers! You find slave catchers in Jefferson City, Simon, sir?"

"Maybe something worse. Mr. Peece thinks as how we might have some turkey rustlers on our trail."

Just then Mr. Peece himself came out of the woods from his morning ablutions. He was folding up his straight-edge razor. His face was all shiny and smooth. "You tell your tale to Jabeth, Simon?"

"Enough of it."

"All right, then. Let's get these turkeys on the road!"

Bidwell Peece had listened chapter and verse to my story the night before. He didn't say aught about the bit where I got gulled. I took that as a personal kindness on his part, since the more I thought about it, the more foolish I felt. Finally I got to the section about Pa and his sudden interest in fatherhood and turkeys.

Mr. Peece stroked his chin. "Mind if I were to offer a little piece of advice, son? Considerin' as how I have been in this world a mite longer than you. And considerin' as how I ain't always been a drunk."

"I never thought you was, Mr. Peece."

"Appreciate that, Simon." He reached for my empty plate and filled it up again. "Them big days of the Santa Fe trail? You mightn't believe it, but I had me my own mule train. Better'n twenty wagons strong. Twice the year I made the trip from Independence.

Took to staying longer and longer on the Santa Fe end, though."

"Why was that, Mr. Peece?"

He scratched at his whiskers. "Had me a sweetheart there. Prettiest little Mexican girl. Married her up and everything." He sighed. "I was a happy man, Simon."

"Had you any youngsters?" I was getting into the story.

"Two boys and a girl. They was sweet, too. Jabbered in American and Spanish both. And the way they'd climb all over me when I got back from months on the trail!"

I didn't think this story was going to have a happy ending, but I needed to find out. "Then what?"

He threw a few more sticks on the fire. "Got back one trip, they was all gone. From the cholera. Ever' last one of them. Took up the bottle about then."

I sighed. "Least you didn't leave *them*, Mr. Peece."

"Only for the job. Would've never abandoned my little family. That's what I was working up to, son. Your pa—" He stopped.

"Needn't dance around it, Mr. Peece."

"Your pa, he don't sound the same kind of heart-broken I was."

"That crossed my mind. It truly did."

Mr. Peece patted at the strands of gray hair atop his head. "So, if you agree with me that far, then you could maybe see to take the whole situation one step further."

"What'd that step be, Mr. Peece?"

"Well, if your pa ain't broken up over you, Simon, you got to stop and think what might be rousing his interest."

I stopped to think. "Turkeys?"

Mr. Peece shook his head sadly. "Not turkeys, Simon. *Dollars.* Five thousand of 'em come Denver."

"Oh." I cogitated that for a piece. "But if he's really needing a little money, I won't begrudge it—"

"Your pa don't sound like the sort to stop at a little, Simon. Don't mean to malign a man I never met, but he sounds more like the sort that'd want the whole lot."

"Oh." I thought some more. "You mean like yours, and mine, and Miss Rogers's—and even Jabeth's if he was to lend us a hand all the way out there."

"I do mean that."

I set down my second helping of stew. Wasn't that hungry anymore. "It's kind of hard to find and lose your pa all in the same day, Mr. Peece."

"I'm full of sympathy, son. I can feel exactly where it hurts."

"What'll we do next?"

"We set off early tomorrow and see what happens. Give the man a second chance. If he don't turn up after us, maybe—just maybe—I be reading the whole thing wrong."

I brightened some. "That'd be a good test, wouldn't it!"

Mr. Peece finished banking the fire for the night. "It sure as shooting would."

But Pa did turn up after us. And he wasn't alone, either.

We'd been working the birds hard on the new road west from Jefferson City, and just managed to herd them safely through the covered bridge over Upper Moreau Creek. We was all taking a little spell of rest on the other side, sort of fluffing up our feathers again preparatory to moving on, when it happened.

Emmett heard the horse hooves clattering over the wooden slats of the bridge first and set into a barking jag. Funny thing about Emmett. He mostly ignored the stray wagon traffic we'd come upon along the road. He had his mind on his work, and rarely even barked at the birds, except to keep them from grief. But his dander was up this time.

Mr. Peece and I got to our feet fast. Jabeth, too. He was sticking close to us today on account of the possible trouble we was halfway expecting. Strange, but even the weather had that anticipatory feel about it. The dawn fog had drifted off the ground, but never did burn away completely. Now the sky was gray and heavy, with wisps of low clouds still settled here and there, particularly around the water. So, as we looked back at that covered bridge, it was interesting to see these two horsemen bursting from the dark tunnel of its mouth. Bursting through the shroud of mists around it, then careening to a halt not yards from our resting place.

I turned to Mr. Peece. He was examining the horses first. It was his way, and it made sense. It was fine horseflesh quivering before us, all snorting and lathered with sweat. Should be. I recognized the animals as two of the fancy Arabians from the circus ring the night before. But my interest was held more by the riders.

"Afternoon, Pa. Mr. Cleaver?" I nodded at the second rider. "Ain't you both going to be missing out on your early circus show in Jefferson City?"

"Simon."

Pa swooped to the ground right graceful. But I wasn't really watching his style. Was more interested in the rifle he had cradled in one arm. And the full packs astride his saddle. Come to notice it, Cleaver the coconut man had full packs, too. And a shiny revolver poking out from where he'd stashed it through a belt beneath his open vest. Seemed like mighty uncomfortable positioning to me, on account of the fact that a man could nullify himself right quick if a gun were to go off with the barrel pointed in that location. I forced my eyes away.

"You contemplating a journey, Pa? Looks like you packed for one."

"Had me a sudden urge to see gold country, Simon."

"Could've took your circus steamboat to Independence easier."

"The steamboat can't go much past Independence. River's too rough. Also, the Missouri don't go as far as Denver."

"Well, I knew that."

Then I just kept jabbering on about nothing in particular, because I wasn't sure what was about to happen next. Also, I didn't feel like rushing into finding out. Mr. Peece, he must've felt the same way, because he was busy calming them nervous, frothing mounts. He looked kind of unhappy at the way Pa and that Cleaver had treated such fine animals.

I turned from the horses to check on how Jabeth was taking events. Strange, but Jabeth was nowheres to be seen. Seemed like he'd just melted himself into the mists coming off of the creek. There being not much more to do, I bent to quiet Emmett.

"Hush, boy. These here men don't mean us no harm."

Emmett felt otherwise. He stopped barking, but his entire body shivered beneath my hands. I could feel the twitching under his skin. And now his teeth was bared. Hadn't ever seen Emmett's teeth bared thataways. I took another moment to try to soothe him, using it as an excuse to do some thinking. Animals was always smarter than most people thought. And

Emmett here was the smartest dog I'd ever had the pleasure of knowing. If Emmett thought Pa and Cleaver was up to mischief—

"Hate to do this, son—"

Too late.

Before I spun away from the dog, Pa had my hands caught behind my back. He was tying them tight with a good long thong of rawhide. Over to the horses, Cleaver had his revolver pointed at Mr. Peece.

"Want me to put this one out of his misery right off, Samson?" he asked. "He's a fairly mangy specimen to begin with."

"Nah," Pa answered, whilst I struggled mightily—and uselessly—in his iron grasp. "Ain't much point, and probably ain't worth the bullet. Just truss him up and haul him into the woods. It'll be a good long while before he gets loose."

Then Pa apparently had another thought. "Might do to gag him, though, in case any Good Samaritan should head this way."

Pa drug me off to the woods, too, after he strung up my legs worse than any squealing hog's. As he was stuffing his huge handkerchief rather tenderly into my mouth, he left me with a few words of fatherly advice.

"Now, don't you be holding this against me, Simon. But the way you skedaddled before dawn, I got the distinct idea you didn't want to share any of your

birds. Not even with your poor, long-lost pa. Me and
Cleaver, we got fed up on the circus round about the
moment I explained your turkey walk. We got to
make some distance now, before my old comrades dis-
cover two of their prize horses has bolted the barn, so
to speak."

He'd finished stuffing and was knotting a red neck-
erchief around the gag and behind my head for good
measure. "You have yourself a fine life, son. Steer away
from confidence games, and don't take no wooden
nickels."

Pa gave me a friendly pat on the head, and was
gone. Shortly thereafter, it started in to rain. Cold
and hard.

"Simon! You all right, Simon?"

I opened my eyes. There was Jabeth hunkering over
me, my bowie knife in his hands and genuine concern
spread across his face.

"Mmmmffgh!" It was all I could manage to say.

"Hang on. I'll get you freed up in two shakes."

And he did. I spit out the gag with relief. "You
didn't call me *sir*! Thank you, Jabeth. Thank you
kindly."

"My pleasure. *Sir.*" But he was grinning with delight as he set to with my arms and legs. Then I was
hobbling up, rubbing at the rawhide burns on my
wrists.

"Never did know my own pa, Simon," Jabeth started in again, "but if they's all like that—"

The topic was a sore one at the moment. I changed the subject. "You find Mr. Peece?"

"Sure did. Ungagged him and he said to take care of you first."

I glanced around some more through the dripping trees. "What about Emmett? They didn't go and take Emmett, too, did they?"

"No way. He's keeping company with Mr. Peece. Already had half of his leg thongs chewed off."

That news relieved me mightily. "All right, then. You just earned you a portion of my enterprise, Jabeth. Always allowing that we get them birds back where they belongs."

He blinked and almost looked insulted. "Ain't rescued you for no reward, Simon. Rescued you 'cause you're my friend. Ain't never had a friend before."

Well, that warmed me as good as Miss Rogers's farewell hug. I shook the cold rain from my head and felt way better.

"You know something, Jabeth? I ain't ever had a friend before, either. But if you want to come to Denver, you still get a share, fair and square."

"Since you puts it like that . . ."

We slapped each other on the back, then set off for Mr. Peece. I figured we had some heavy thinking to do.

❧ EIGHT ❧

Now, as I see it," Mr. Peece was saying, "we got a couple things on our side."

The three of us and Emmett was huddled under a lean-to of branches and leaves we'd cobbled together against the rain still falling fast and furious. A little fire sputtered bravely before us, and we was warming our hands by it. Unfortunately, our hands was the only things going to get warmed this night. Between the weather and the early darkness, even Jabeth hadn't been able to catch us supper.

"What might they be? Those things on our side?" I asked.

Jabeth shivered between us, but gave Mr. Peece a hopeful look.

"First off," my drover says, "your pa and that Cleaver person don't expect us to be unbound this quick. Nor do they expect us to be pursuing them. They just took it for plumb natural that we'd give up entire."

Mr. Peece held out a second finger. "Next, they don't look like the sort to know a blamed thing about turkeys. After the way they treated that fine horse-flesh—"

"You think they's likely to destroy my birds?" I worried aloud. "Miss Rogers, she's counting on me to get them straight through to Denver. All one thousand of 'em. And—"

"There's bound to be some loss, Simon," Mr. Peece cut in. "Even without extry-ordinary circumstances. And we got us some extry-ordinary circumstances right now."

"And it's all my fault," I mourned. "If I hadn't of wanted to see them lions and tigers and camels the way I did—"

"Don't you go berating yourself, Simon. It was a true educational urge. Ain't ever nothing wrong with one of them." Mr. Peece absently petted Emmett in his lap. "But there's always a surprise tucked away some-wheres. And your pa turned into a very wild one indeed."

Jabeth shifted to get his bare feet closer to the flames. "Tell us some more about what we got going for us, Mr. Peece, sir. I needs to know."

Bidwell Peece smiled. What remaining teeth he had flashed real nice. "Why, we got *you*, Jabeth. They don't know about you atall."

After Jabeth finished beaming, Mr. Peece wrapped

up our planning session. "Now, I think we all ought to get us some sleep. Come first light, we catch up with them rustlers. Sneaky, like. Don't let 'em know we's about. We'll do things extemporaneous from there."

It wasn't any hardship rising early in the morning. I was stiff all over from the damp and cold and not having near enough sleep on account of the drips of water that'd hit me regular through our roof during the night. I missed my blankets and I missed my breakfast. Most of all, I missed the comforting gobbles of my turkeys. Who'd have thought a blood father could take all that away from his only son? Aunt Maybelle's railing about Pa over the years came back to me. Least she'd been correct about that one thing. I stretched to rid my mind of the thought and turned to my companions.

"Hey, Jabeth!" My friend seemed able to sleep through anything. I gave him a gentle boot. "Mr. Peece? Time to turn out and move on."

We loped down the center of the muddy road to warm ourselves. For a comfort, at least the rain had slowed to a misty drizzle. After about a mile, we passed a lone, deserted-looking farmhouse. I saw Jabeth perk up and start paying attention.

"You see some breakfast lying about, Jabeth?" I

asked, sort of jocular like. Didn't really expect an answer, but Jabeth, he broke into a sprint. Then he yelled back.

"Come and get it!"

Emmett reached him first, then me. By the time Mr. Peece puffed up, Jabeth already had me hanging on to the horns of an old brown cow. Lowing something pitiful, she was. Small wonder, since she badly needed milking.

"We're gonna do us a good deed all around," Jabeth said. "But first I'll need your hat, Mr. Peece, sir."

Mr. Peece clamped on to his old slouch topper fast. "My hat? What on earth for?"

He looked at Jabeth, then studied the cow. Slowly it began to dawn on him.

"*No.* Why, no way am I going to—" He kept spluttering, hanging on to that hat. "This headgear and me, we's gone through hell and beyond together. How'd you expect me to—"

Jabeth held out his hand, patient and expectant both.

Mr. Peece gave up on his hat. Slowly.

In a few minutes the old cow was almost sighing with relief. And we were taking turns drinking our fill of warm milk from that very disreputable article. When we couldn't swallow any more, Emmett got his turn. That dog was so appreciative, he licked out every last drop, then picked up the brim between his teeth and trotted the hat back to his master.

"What'd you expect me to do with this now?" Mr. Peece crumpled the soggy felt in his hands. Disgust shone all over his face.

"Put it back where it belongs." I laughed. "We might need it again come dinnertime."

It wasn't but another mile along that we saw the first signs of my deepest fears. One lone bronze turkey was straggling down the road, looking as lost as ever he could be.

I whistled, then set in to making a little turkey small talk. That tom trots right up to me. I swear, I never saw such a grateful look in any bird's beady eyes. I fondled his miserable, wet feathers, the whole yard from his neck to the tip of his tail. "Look sharp, Jabeth, Mr. Peece. We may be closing in on the rascals."

Come midafternoon, the sun had broken through the clouds with a kind of milky light that reminded me of breakfast. By this time, Emmett was feeling much better. So were the rest of us. We'd rounded up near a hundred of my birds. They'd been found in dribs and drabs: forlorn in trees; pecking despondently by the side of the road. Jabeth even fetched one from the very mouth of a fox. Got him a nice fox pelt in the bargain, and the turkey's neck not even broken yet, either.

I began to feel a little sorry for my pa. If this was the way he intended to make his fortune, he'd find himself in Denver with only about a dozen turkeys for his trouble. Mr. Peece must have been considering the same thing, because he inspected our little flock and grinned.

"At the rate we're going, boys, all we'll have to do is stay a few steps behind the rogues. In a day or two, we'll have us all our birds back in hand!"

"But not the wagon and supplies," I reminded him. "Not to mention Sparky, and the rest of my fine mules."

Jabeth flipped my bowie knife as graceful as one of Miss Lila's turns on that flying swing. "Only thing concerns me is the guns they got. I don't take to guns—when they's in somebody else's hands."

"Me neither," I agreed.

"Got to catch 'em when their guns is elsewhere," Mr. Peece reckoned. "Maybe while they're asleep?"

"Now, that's an idea!" I continued down the road. "Take left flank, Emmett. But don't hurry 'em too hard now. We don't want to turn a bend and bump into my pa."

We waited till our little flock was roosted comfortably for the night in a small patch of woods, then set off along the next piece of road. Two miles before that we'd got through the village of Russellville, practically on the tails of Pa and Cleaver. At least, that's what the local folks said when they sees us coming. But they said it from behind curtained windows and doors just barely ajar.

"You with them other turkey people?"

That was a sort of a whisper, and I had to hunt around to find where it came from. It was a small boy peeking out the crack of a door.

"Not on your life! We're after 'em for stealing my birds!"

"Ain't you got no guns?"

"Don't believe in guns."

A communal sigh issued forth from the houses, and heads started poking out. First slowly, then with indignation.

"They was waving them weapons around most dangerous!"

"That slim, gambler-looking fellow, he shoots his off! Just 'cause my boy helped himself to one of them birds. Lord knows there was enough!"

I swiveled around right quick to make certain Emmett and Jabeth had our flock strictly in hand. They did. "So how many'd you get from the villains?" I asked, casual like.

A giggle came from a window farther down the street. "About half a dozen! All big 'uns! After the way they was acting, we figured them birds was fair game."

"Russellville's feasting tonight!" said someone else with a laugh.

"Still like to get my hands on them fellows, feast or not," concluded another hidden body.

After those final comments, I herded my troops

along the main and only street with considerable more energy. Granted, these folks had been pressed some, but it didn't strike me that the good people of Russellville was entirely ethical. Not by a long shot. I was sincerely happy to see the end of that village and its two churches.

I was still fuming over those lost six birds when we'd bedded the others and set off for Pa and Cleaver. After all we'd gone through this far, to have my stock disappear thataways! Why, six turkeys was worth . . . I figured on exactly what they was worth for near a mile. It'd just come to me when Emmett let out a growl.

Mr. Peece clamped a hand on the dog's muzzle fast. "Ssh. They must be dead ahead!"

There was a hill in front of us, with a line of trees skirting the road. Beyond was nothing but tall grass. I bolted into the grass fast. Jabeth and Mr. Peece followed. We snuck up the hill on our bellies, then spied down on a campsite.

The last of the day's hazy sun floated over the other nine hundred or so of my turkeys that was scratching out sleeping nests amidst the tall grass surrounding the supply wagon. And there was Sparky and Snowball and my other mules grazing peacefully alongside them prize Arabians. My, but it was a solace to set eyes on them all again.

It was a perfect scene, aside from the fact that none

of it belonged to me at the moment, the way it should have. I cast my eyes back to the western sky. Now the sun was disappearing into a bank of dark clouds. There'd be light for another hour, maybe, no thanks to the pitiful attempts at a fire Pa and Cleaver was busy concocting in the center of the camp down below.

They went at it like they'd never had need to start one before. And they was arguing up a storm the entire time. They sure was a blight on the beauties of beasts and nature in general.

"You're so ready to use that revolver of yours, Cleaver, how is it you didn't wing one of them villagers when they went after our birds?" Pa was griping.

"Shut your mouth, Samson. I was doing the best I could. It ain't easy being cowherd to a bunch of stupid turkeys!"

"I should say not! You been letting them slip through your fingers the livelong day!"

"All the while *you* were driving the wagon. The easy job!"

"We flipped on that up front, Cleaver. Is it my fault I got heads this morning?"

"And yesterday afternoon, too. It's against the law of averages. I'd like to see that dollar you flipped with, Samson. Both sides. If it ain't two-headed, I'll eat my—"

The thigh-thick, sopping branch what Pa was balancing on his shoulder swung dangerously close to Cleaver's head. "You accusing me of cheating, Cleaver? Thought *you* was the expert in that department."

Cleaver ducked and backed off. He must have set his gun down somewheres, otherwise I knew it would be pointing at my pa this very instant.

"Got to cool that temper of yours, Samson Green."

Pa shifted his load again threateningly. "Look who's talking, Mr.—"

Cleaver backed some more and tried on a little weasel smile. "Why don't I just fetch that side of bacon I found in the wagon, Samson? It's been a long day. A good, hot supper and everything'll look better."

"Won't look no better till we hit Denver," Pa concluded. "How that simple-minded boy of mine got as far as Jefferson City with this freakish animal show is beyond me. Skittering turkeys, mules what hates my guts . . ."

Pa finally set down the five-foot branch and fished out a matchbox. Next to me, Jabeth was convulsing himself with laughter he was trying to swallow. "He thinks he's gonna set that, that *Yule* log afire with a match?" he whispered.

I cracked a grin, too. "Don't know where exactly my pa's been all the rest of his life," I said, "but I guess the circus don't teach you no useful skills."

.   .   .

Pa and Cleaver finally gave up on the fire and attacked my side of bacon raw. Next they both smoked a cigar, glaring at each other across the unlit fire the entire time. By then it had gone full dark and it was hard to see aught but the glowing tips of those cheroots. But a body could *feel* those glares passing between the two, even way up here on the hill. At last, without another word, they both wrapped up in blankets for the night.

"Sleep well, Pa," I murmured. " 'Cause it's gonna be a short rest for you and Cleaver."

By the time the snores from the camp below started drifting up our hill, Mr. Peece was already adding to them. I let him nap a good hour, since I knew he could use it. Then I nudged Jabeth.

"You ready?"

"Rarin' to go." Jabeth grinned. He was already flashing my bowie knife. If there was a moon, that blade'd be blazing up a storm.

"Mr. Peece?" I turned to the drover.

"Umph?" His eyes shot open.

"We're heading down to camp now. Can you keep Emmett quiet?"

He shifted up on his elbows from the damp grass. "I'll carry him. Should do the trick."

"Fine. You three stand watch over Cleaver, whilst I attend to my pa." I was already unwinding the length of Pa's rawhide that I'd had wrapped around my waist since being rescued yesterday.

"Sure you can handle him yourself, son? The man's got prodigious strength."

"I got me some of that strength, too, Mr. Peece. Plus some righteous anger. I figure I owe it to Pa to even accounts between us."

"You got a point, Simon. Good luck to us all."

It turned out way easier than I expected. Pa's rifle was lying by his head, and first thing I did was quietly move it out of range. As he was sleeping on his belly, all I did next was set a knee into his back, add a little weight, and grab for his flapping arms. His roar of outrage like to wake the dead—and the livestock, too.

"*Damnation!* What devilish fiend is a-climbing my back?"

"Rest easy, Pa. It's only Simon, your simpleminded son."

My fingers were already making quick work with the rawhide knots I was constructing around his wrists.

"I hate to do this, Pa. It hurts me real bad. But you didn't leave me no choice."

In a moment I was throwing off the blankets and hog-tying Pa's wrists to his ankles. Had to turn around and sit on him to accomplish that, though. All the time, Pa was writhing and spouting a lot of words that would've turned Miss Rogers gray premature. Aunt Maybelle, too.

I fished in my pocket and pulled out the huge handkerchief. "Got something here that belongs to you, Pa. Thought you might like it back."

I turned Pa over and began stuffing the gag down his throat. Maybe not quite as tender as he'd done the job on me a day earlier. "It ain't necessarily a sign of manliness to talk such talk, Pa. Brave actions and a gentle heart—"

Pa started in thumping his entire body with violence. I had to stomp on him a little more.

"—Miss Rogers always said as how those was the things that truly made a man."

My eyes caught Pa's through the darkness. They was glaring like that there tiger's back at the circus. With sheer anger and frustration. I guess mine glared a little right back before I raised my head from my efforts at last. "How you people doing over there?"

Mr. Peece had finally released Emmett, and the dog had Cleaver's pistol hand firmly between his teeth. My, but he had spunk for such a little critter. Jabeth was starting with the other rawhide rope from the feet up, and my drover was happily gagging the coconut man.

"This'll fix you for holding a gun to me," he was saying. "I been scorned and spat upon, but in my day no man held a gun to Bidwell Peece!"

I let the boys finish up with their fun, then checked

the bonds. They was good and strong. Finally, Mr. Peece seemed to notice me.

"What next, Simon? How do we dispose of them so's they won't get back into our hair right quick?"

"Got some ideas about that, Mr. Peece. I truly do. But first things first." I bent over Cleaver and felt for his pockets. Nothing there. Then I thought to try his belt.

"What you doing, Simon?" Jabeth asked. "We ain't no thieves!"

"Not by a long shot." A grin spread over my face as I felt the thickness of the belt. I split it open and out spilled coins. "But Pa and Cleaver owe me for six turkeys, Denver price. Also for a few more that probably strayed past us during the day. And I already turned out Pa's pockets. They was sheer empty, aside from that double-headed silver dollar of his. I let him keep that, as he might be needing it down the road, the way his luck's been turning."

I began counting the five-dollar gold pieces. "Six of these would make thirty dollars. That's for Russellville's turkey feast." I looked up. "I want to be fair, Mr. Peece. And you ain't got as much invested as me. What you figure I should have beyond?"

Mr. Peece bent to finger the pile. "I was counting them nesting birds in the sunset, Simon. Seems like another fifteen gold pieces ought to cover the damage."

I completed the transaction and got to my feet.

"All right, then. Mr. Peece, you and Emmett stay on here at the main camp for the night. Jabeth and me are going to load up the mules with these gentlemen and give them a ride back to Russellville. The folks there expressed some interest in meeting up with them again."

While Jabeth grinned in anticipation, I glanced around the campsite, sorting out the last arrangements in my mind. "The only other thing to decide about is those prize horses. Should I be leaving them in Russellville with Pa and Cleaver, Mr. Peece?"

He rubbed at a cheek. "I don't know, Simon. On the one hand, it'd be just like putting temptation smack into your Pa's hands again. On the other, those Russellville folks are just as likely to latch on to the horses themselves. Considerin' their record for high principles."

"I'd sure hate to have the circus people accuse *us* of rustling, Mr. Peece. In case they ever came looking for that horseflesh."

"We didn't open any barn doors, Simon, no matter how you look at it. And it's a fine breeding pair. I'm thinking they'll go for a decent price in Denver if we was to treat 'em right along the way. Then again, they'd make a good start to somebody's establishment, if he was considering starting a ranching-type establishment out that ways—"

Mr. Peece stopped, then started in again. "Mules is fine creatures in and of themselves, but you got to admit, Simon . . . you got to admit they ain't got no breeding future whatsoever!"

That being possibly the longest speech I ever heard from Mr. Peece it took a moment to work around its ramifications—aside from the obvious fact any fool knew, which was that mules couldn't make young'uns. The bottom line was that Mr. Peece was already in love with those prize Arabians. I could see his feelings clear through the night's darkness. I nodded and spun away.

"Fine. We'll take a chance with the horses. Meanwhile, Jabeth and me, we'll stop the night with the other birds and see you here in the morning. Then," I finished, "then we can move on to Denver."

Mr. Peece smiled with evident relief. "Couldn't have planned it better myself, son."

❦ NINE ❧

It was a joyous meeting of the flocks the next morning. My birds acted like they was genuinely delighted to see each other again. Especially the lost toms, the way they was strutting and fanning their fine tails to catch the attentions of their admiring hens. Mr. Peece had done up a glorious breakfast, too. While the birds socialized and we gorged, more plans were worked out.

"I figure we can make it to Versailles sometime tomorrow, Simon," Mr. Peece said. "That there's the biggest town we're likely to come across before Denver, outside of Independence. Might be wise to top up our supplies with a little of Cleaver's money."

Those coins were clanking around in my pockets; had been all morning on the short haul to main camp. "Work up a list, Mr. Peece. I might have a few things to add to it."

I knew right off what was chief among that list, too. Watching Jabeth do his scarecrow imitation to one side of the small flock this morning had settled his main problem in my mind. It had to do with his *feet*. There he was, kind of mincing hither and yon, flapping like usual.

"Jabeth?" I said.

"Yes, Simon?"

"How is it you don't walk funny like that 'cept when you're working the birds?"

He stopped cold in his tracks. A hangdog expression spread over his face. "Don't like to mention something so silly, Simon."

"Spit it out, Jabeth. You're among friends."

Well, his head was still drooping, nearly down to his splayed bare toes. "I'm learning to love your turkeys better every day, Simon. Truly I am."

"But?" I pushed him along.

"But . . ." Then he finally spit it out. Fast. "But I hate like blazes to have to squish through fresh turkey droppings, Simon!"

So that was it! It didn't take me no time at all to grasp the situation. Before you know it, I'm slapping my knees, roaring. Near to rolling in them identical droppings. Jabeth, he didn't see the humor of it the way I did.

"You got *boots*, Simon."

I caught myself long enough to stare down my body. So I did. Yet I chuckled on and off the last half mile to Mr. Peece's breakfast anyhow, and kept on chuckling through the meal.

The next day we left the flock just outside Versailles with Mr. Peece and Emmett. Jabeth and I headed past the outlying wheat fields in to town. Still being in slave territory—though not north of the Missouri River in Little Dixie where most of the owners lived—Jabeth hunched into his toadeating act and started treating me to his *master* nonsense again. He shuffled a few steps behind me. He bowed and scraped. It grated. But as it was for his own long-term good, I put up with it.

After perambulating the town, we settled on the biggest general store, where Jabeth trailed me inside. I guess we didn't look that flush, because nobody paid us any mind. I cleared my throat a few times to no effect. Then I started in losing patience. I raised my voice a little.

"Need to look at some boots."

At last the storekeeper glanced up from his ledger books and down to my feet. "For you? Don't know as we stock 'em that big."

"Nope. For my boy here."

A look of scorn passed across the man's face. "Ain't got slave grade here."

"Don't want slave grade. Want a good, solid pair of boots so's I won't have to be reshodding him for a long while."

He perked up. "If that's the case . . ."

Poor Jabeth had some time getting fitted. First off

I had to buy him socks, so's his black feet wouldn't contaminate the stock. Then he hobbled around in half a dozen pair, looking like maybe the boot idea was a poor one to begin with. I finally bent over to where he was prodding at a toe cap.

"Ain't you ever had boots before, Jabeth?" I whispered.

"Never!" he tossed back. "And I'm beginning to wonder if they's worth all the fuss. *Master.*"

"Watch your tongue, boy," I said in a louder tone. "Else you won't get that new shirt I promised!"

"New shirt?" That sparked up Jabeth considerable. He hobbled around a little more. "Think these'll do fine, master sir. Just need to break 'em in."

We left our grocery order piled on the floor, ready to fetch when we walked the flock through town the next morning. What we carried out was Jabeth's old rags, done up in a parcel as if they were the finest silk cloth. That shopkeeper had finally stood up and saluted to the color of my money.

As for Jabeth, he was sporting new togs from top to bottom and inside out, with extra drawers and even an extra shirt for when the first batch got too stiff with dirt to wear. I'd bought me a few extras on that account, too. Uncle Lucas hadn't exactly set me loose from the farm in style.

I'd also invested in a new bowie knife, to replace the one on permanent loan to Jabeth. Besides a tin plate and cup and blanket to complete Jabeth's kit, the final purchase pleased me mightily. It was a spanking new slouch hat for Mr. Peece.

We started to walk back to the turkeys in high spirits. A barbershop stopped me in my tracks. I took a look at Jabeth's halo of tight curls, then felt the length of my own thatch.

"One more stop, Jabeth."

I sank into the barber's chair first. I hadn't ever been in one before, Aunt Maybelle always having done the honors with her mixing bowl and sewing scissors. It was a novelty having a towel slung across my shoulders, and the barber standing there stropping his razors.

"What'll it be?" he asked. "Wash, cut, and shave?"

I felt my roughened cheeks and grinned. "Why not?"

Mr. Peece like to faint when he saw the two of us strutting back into camp.

"What in tarnation . . . what you fellas gone and done to yourselves?"

I turned full before him. Hadn't recognized myself, either, when that Versailles barber dusted me all down with sweet-smelling talc and held a little mirror to my face. A new and different Simon Green had stared back at me. I swore off mixing-bowl haircuts then and there for the rest of my natural life. Still, it was nice to know the old Simon was underneath it all.

"How about Jabeth, here, Mr. Peece?" I twirled my

friend for good measure. Jabeth, he hadn't needed the shave, and the cut took about three inches off his height, but I thought he ended up right handsome in the process. Between that and the new duds that didn't flap, of course. "Approve of the effect, Mr. Peece?"

"Think I'll just go hide out with the mules," the skinner answered. "Ain't nobody gonna give me a second look next to you two blades."

"I think they might, at that," I said, and pulled his new hat from behind my back.

"What's this?" Mr. Peece reached for the present, then dropped his fingers.

"Ain't it time, Mr. Peece? You been looking for a new life, haven't you? Seems to me as if a new hat fits right in with a new life."

He finally accepted my present. He fingered the clean black felt for a long moment. At last he swung off the old article and clapped on the new. "Man don't need a drink anymore when he's got friends as good as you, Simon," was all he said. Then he stomped off to the mules.

The next few days we made good time through more wheat country to the village of Cole Camp, where we swung north along what Mr. Peece said was the last section of dirt road for a ways. Mr. Peece knew his roads from his droving days along the Santa Fe Trail, and afterward taking wagons on shorter hauls around Missouri. That twenty-mile stretch due north was a nice piece to travel, on account of it following the Spring Fork, which gave the birds all the water they wanted.

It was truly amazing how much a turkey could drink. They was pretty good about trotting along most of the day. But when they decided it was time to stop, they wanted plenty to drink, then plenty to eat before settling for the night. We got to talking about exactly *how much* they could drink one evening around the campfire.

"Well," Mr. Peece considered, "strikes me that a medium bird could down a couple quarts of water a day easy."

"More," Jabeth threw in. "Three quarts. End of the day, you're always tending to the four-legged animals, Mr. Peece, sir. I don't think you pay that much mind to the turkeys."

"Do too!" Mr. Peece said that like he'd been insulted.

"I'd have to go along with Jabeth on this one, Mr. Peece." I tossed the skeleton of a trout from my plate and reached into the frypan for another helping of Jabeth's catch. "I'd go as high as a gallon, myself."

That got Mr. Peece's ire up. "A gallon! We hit Sedalia tomorrow, where the road ends and we head due west again?"

"Yes?"

"You be willing to put out a few coins for a little testing device—"

"What sort of testing device?" Jabeth interrupted. "I don't see how a person can measure what a turkey drinks. Nohow."

"A very simple device." Mr. Peece grinned. "And not a total waste of funds, either, as it'll have long-term uses for all of us, man and beast alike."

"Come on, Mr. Peece." He'd got me wondering now. "What exactly is it you've got in mind?"

But Mr. Peece only grinned some more and turned in for the night.

So the next morning we set off with a little more vigor and anticipation in our steps than usual. Jabeth and I, we was mighty curious about what Bidwell Peece was holding up his sleeve. But when we finally got to Sedalia, Mr. Peece just stretched out his hand, palm up. I crossed it with a coin and he disappeared into the one and only store.

Meanwhile, there was Jabeth and Emmett and me and the birds clogging the dusty little road through town. Naturally, we 'roused some interest from the local folks. All of them, seems like. They stood around gaping, but saying nothing until my drover emerged again, his hands full.

"Why that's nothing but a ten-gallon copper wash-tub, Mr. Peece!"

"Correct, Simon."

"Like my mama did all the laundry in," Jabeth added.

"Yup," Mr. Peece verified. "What you boys figure is the key part of that description you just give me?"

Well, Jabeth and I both scratched our heads over that one. Jabeth spoke up first.

"The *ten-gallon* part?"

"Give that boy a cee-gar!"

Mr. Peece cackled like a madman all the way to the town pump. There he commenced to fill the tub with water. Right up to the very brim. Then he waved us over. "Clear a little space between the birds, Jabeth. You haul this to the space, Simon. Mind you don't spill a drop!"

I followed his directions, shaking my head the entire time. Had that spanking new hat done something to Mr. Peece's brainpower? The villagers came closer, surrounding us. One of the men finally spoke.

"You fellas got a little bet going here? Looks like a bet to me."

Another man shot out a spurt of tobacco juice. "Iffen it be a proper bet, like to get in on it. Ain't been no action around here in a coon's age."

Mr. Peece trotted front and center, eyes twinkling. "Certainly, gentlemen. You're all welcome to partake of our little wager. A nickel'll get you in. But let me explain first. This"—he waved at the tub—"this is a ten-gallon copper washtub. You all agreed on that?"

Solemn head-nodding began.

"Right. And it's filled to the very brim with water. Fresh, pure spring water from your very own fine village well. Ten gallons of it."

More nods.

Next Mr. Peece pointed toward my flock. "Those are turkeys. Nearly one thousand of the finest, top-notch *bronze* turkeys. Our wager is simple. We're just trying to figure how much a hale and hearty turkey can drink in a sitting. My estimate is two quarts each. My associates"—he pointed at Jabeth and me—"they figure three quarts and one gallon respectively. Got all that?"

More nodding and a little head-scratching from the crowd, which had expanded even more by this time. The bartender from the saloon on the far side of the street must've lost his customers, 'cause he dragged out a table and set a few bottles and glasses onto it. Then he went back to haul out a couple of chairs.

"How you gonna prove it?" a broad, bearded gent finally asked.

Mr. Peece smiled. "Simple, my good sir. We set ten turkeys to the tub. We let them drink their fill. Then we see what's left. Closest bets to the three estimates share the pot."

"I'm in." The first nickel got tossed onto the ground. "For two quarts."

"Me, too!" Another nickel followed, starting a second pile. "For three quarts."

"I'm betting with that big fella!"

My head jerked up at the new voice. It was a *lady* placing the bet! She was leaning out the open window over the saloon, sort of dressed like Miss Lila back at the circus. Least, the part of her I could see. She tossed a coin down to me.

"Here you go, big boy!"

I caught it. "A whole quarter, ma'am?"

"I put my money on winners." She laughed, and so did the bartender and other gentlemen, who were now heading for the bottles.

I carefully started a third pile, then stared at Mr. Peece. Who'd have thought he had this whole project in him? Why, he could teach a few things to Cleaver the coconut man! I stepped over to Jabeth.

"Guess we'd better catch ten birds." I leaned a little closer. "And make 'em big ones, Jabeth!"

Turned out Jabeth and I didn't have to do all the work. Those locals, they joined in the game with glee. Pretty soon there was Jabeth and me kneeling in the dirt just outside the brim of the full tub, holding a fat tom each. Eight of the men was each hanging on to a bird, too. The turkeys already smelled the water and had their necks stretched, bright red wattles convulsing in anticipation.

Above us, Mr. Peece was grinning to beat the band.

"Now, I'm about to count to three," he said. "On the count of three, I swoops off my hat. That's when you all set loose the birds."

We waited. The crowd edging around us did, too.

"One."

Mr. Peece was having the time of his life.

"Two."

He was stretching it for all it was worth.

"Three!"

Off swooped the new hat with a flourish. Down plopped the birds, panting for the water.

I got to my feet and backed off a ways. But not too far. So did everyone else. But we're standing there in silence under the hot sun, nobody saying anything for fear of putting the turkeys off their drinks.

After a while, you could see the difference in the tub's water level. That water was noticeably disappearing by the inch. My birds didn't stop. They leaned over the rim, brown legs and claws stretched tense behind them. They just kept on dipping their beaks into the coolness, and guzzling the liquid down their long throats. When the water got below the halfway mark, Jabeth poked me.

"I never knowed watching turkeys could be so interesting!"

I glanced around at the men, the lady above the saloon, the rest of the village. It was as if the whole place was under some kind of spell. The remainder of my flock, too. They was straining their necks, wattles and snoods throbbing, eyes cocked toward the tub, trying to figure what was happening. I smiled.

104

"*I* knew birds was interesting all along, Jabeth."

Finally there came a long sigh from everyone, then a great cheer. Those ten turkeys was waddling away from the tub, bloated. They just up and left. I walked closer and peeked in. Wasn't hardly a drop of water left. They'd drunk it all.

"Whoo-ee!" I yelled. "I was right! That makes a good gallon each!"

There was some back slapping followed by the division of the pot. That lady over the saloon had done all right, after all. I did, too. I made enough in the wager to pay for the original tub. It hadn't been a bad investment after all. Way better than playing around with coconut shells. I turned to Mr. Peece. He was standing there, rubbing his chin.

"Well, Mr. Peece?"

"Well, Simon," he answered. "I was just figuring on whether the turkeys could go for more water, after all. If we was to set *five* birds to the ten gallons—"

I gave my drover a friendly shove. "One time is fun, Mr. Peece. I'm not after pressing our luck, or our birds." Then I grinned, so's he'd know I was overall pleased with him. "And I'm not sure exactly how I feel about traveling with a *gambling* man—"

Mr. Peece, he only cackled a final time. Then he clapped his new hat atop his head. "Let's move out the turkeys, boys, before they roost in the middle of Sedalia's main street."

℘ TEN ℘

Things kind of went smooth then for a while—past Independence, which we steered clear of, and into the Kansas Territory. Funny thing about Jabeth as we got nearer and nearer to that territory. He got jumpier than a bullfrog in high croaking season.

"Mr. Peece, sir," he kept hounding the man at every opportunity. "Are we there yet?"

"Well," Mr. Peece would answer. "First off, we got to get past Westport."

"Then? After Westport? Will there be some line? Sort of a mark across the road to point out the end of Missouri and slave land, and the start of freedom?"

"Ain't exactly like that, Jabeth," Mr. Peece went on. "The prairie just kind of continues, one step pretty much the same as the last. Till we get into Indian country."

"Indian country?" That got my attention right enough. "Never have seen no Indians my entire life."

"That's on account of how the enlightened state of Missouri kicked 'em all out some years back, Simon. Sent 'em farther West. Government told 'em there'd be new lands there for them to hold forever."

"And?" I asked.

Mr. Peece sighed. "Well, now, *forever* in the mind of Indians and *forever* in the mind of white folks seems to be two entire separate things."

"Enough about Indians," Jabeth butted in. "When we gonna be in freedom country?"

We hit the tiny village of Shawnee and moved on through. Once more on the open prairie at the other side, Mr. Peece slowed the mules and glanced down at Jabeth.

"That's it," he said.

"What's it, Mr. Peece, sir?"

"Why, Shawnee. It's as close as I can come to an exact marking line. Shawnee's in Kansas Territory for sure."

"You mean . . ." Jabeth stood stock still in the middle of the dusty road a long moment. Then he hitched up in his newly broken-in boots and went for a mighty leap.

"I'm in *freedom* country! I'm *free*! A *free* man!"

It felt kind of curious watching Jabeth's enthusiasm over something I'd never thought much about before meeting my new friend. What if it was me in his boots? Well, I suppose I'd be mighty relieved, too. I guess Mr. Peece figured the same, because pretty soon Jabeth had dragged him from his perch on the wagon seat and the three of us was dancing around and back-slapping to high heaven. It took us a while to settle down. Then we had to calm Emmett, who'd gone into a rare barking fit due to our antics. Next we had to re-gather the flock, which'd taken flight in fright, also over our unexpected enthusiasm.

It was worth it, just the same. Jabeth, he had a silly grin plastered over his face straight into the evening. Added a couple inches to his height, too, he was walking that tall. And that's the way we traveled for the next few days, straight along the narrow, gritty trail that passed for a highway into Indian country. I was really waiting on my first sight of Indians. Didn't care how ferocious they looked. The wilder the better, far as I was concerned. I'd already met enough so-called civilized folks.

This particular piece of land we was headed for be-longed to the Pottawattomie, Mr. Peece said, although there was some Shawnee and Kaw and Fox toward the south. The Pottawattomie were supposed to be a peaceful sort of people who hunted a little, and farmed a little, and did whatever else was necessary to keep body and soul together.

"What do they hunt for, Mr. Peece?" I asked one evening as we was settling into camp.

"Why, buffalo, Simon."

I stared long and hard over the wild, endless prairie spreading around us. "Ain't seen anything like a buffalo. Nothing like the pictures in Miss Rogers's book. You sure they're still about, Mr. Peece? Sure they ain't all been done in by settlers and such?"

Mr. Peece swiped at some dust on his cheek. "Well, I'll tell you. In the old days, they was thick as flies in these parts. Going south from Independence on the Santa Fe Trail, why, we counted on 'em to keep us in meat. The Indians did, too. They could take a buffalo and strip it down till there was nothing left but the fleas. Made their houses and clothing and blankets from the skins, ate the meat, used the bones for tools. Wasn't enough leavings when they was done to tempt even a hungry vulture."

I considered that information. "Sounds like a useful sort of animal."

"It was. I hope it still is."

Jabeth had been listening the entire time. Meanwhile he was polishing up his bowie knife. He looked up now with a gleam in his eye. "Think I could get me one with this knife?"

Mr. Peece cut a grin. "You see a buffalo with only that in your hand, Jabeth, you turn and run the other way. Fast."

"Why, how big could one be?"

"*Big*. Furry and horned. And mean once their dander's up. Only thing'll take one down is a rifle."

Jabeth glanced toward the wagon where my pa's

rifle was still stashed, along with Cleaver's revolver and their packs—all untouched since the day we'd acquired them. "Maybe it be time to start learning about guns."

"Buffalo steak." Mr. Peece licked his lips. "Liver for strength. Marrow soup. I could maybe get past my own gun feelings for that. Always used to tote one in the old days, anyhow . . ."

"Why'd you stop, Mr. Peece?" I asked.

He gazed on me sorrowfully. "Too much strong drink and guns don't go together, son. A man loses his perspective. Starts to let off a little steam. Pretty soon, somebody gets hurt." He stopped. "Gave up guns when I took to serious drinking. Least I had enough sense for that."

Jabeth was listening to all this, with an expression on his face as if gears and wheels were turning and clicking. "So you do know how to make them work? Guns?"

"Well, I should think so—"

"And you been stone-cold sober the entire time we been acquainted!"

Mr. Peece rubbed at his chin. "I guess that's true."

Jabeth carefully resheathed his knife. "That being the case, any reason why you couldn't give me some shooting lessons, Mr. Peece, sir?"

"Lots. None of which I intends to go into now."

And that's all we could get out of Mr. Peece on the subject of guns that entire night.

The first shooting lesson commenced just past dawn the next morning. That was after Jabeth and I woke up and continued our badgering campaign. Mr. Peece was every bit as reluctant to do it, using his fear of scaring the turkeys as an excuse once he couldn't get past the fact that he was undoubtedly more sober than he'd been in fifteen years.

"Fifteen years?" That figure he'd let out caught my interest. "You mean it was exactly fifteen years ago you lost your loved ones?"

Mr. Peece nodded sadly.

"Ain't it strange that was happening right about the time I was being born?"

"Don't see what that's got to do with anything, Simon."

"Can't be positive, but it seems like more than co-incidence to me, Mr. Peece. The Lord took away, but He was giving back at the same time. Only it was fif-teen years till all of us got together. Almost like a real family. You, and me, and Jabeth here—" I swung to-ward my friend. "Ain't you about fifteen, too?"

"Born in '45, my mama always said."

"So there!" I turned back to Mr. Peece triumphantly.

"So *what*?" he complained. "Fond as I am of you two boys, I can't say I see much logic behind your way of thinking."

I didn't bother asking what *logic* meant. Just pro-ceeded right along. I'd dreamed of buffalo the night before—huge, horned, and hairy—and the whole business was now rousing my interest in rifles as much as Jabeth's.

"So you got at least *part* of a family back, Mr. Peece. And you ain't even looked crosswise at a saloon last few towns we passed through. Seems to me your perspective's right back where it belongs." I stopped for a breath and summed up. "Which means there's no reason in this world you can't give Jabeth and me a few shooting lessons."

Mr. Peece slung his hat onto the ground and growled. "I give up. Fetch the weapon."

We left Emmett guarding the waking flock and tramped through a section of waist-high prairie grass till we figured we was far enough from camp so the birds wouldn't be skittered. The trees had been thinning out remarkably the last few days of the journey, and the only thing stretching around us was miles of flattish prairie and one lone cottonwood next to a creek.

"Here," Mr. Peece said. "As there ain't no other targets at hand, we'll have to settle on that there tree."

Jabeth already had his hand stretched out for the rifle. Mr. Peece swatted it away. "First you got to learn about the basics. Loading and proper handling."

"Why?" Jabeth was annoyed. He was itching to start shooting that poor little tree away, leaf by leaf.

"Because guns ain't no joke. And I don't intend to

be blown from this life premature. Not after it just started getting interesting again."

Mr. Peece proceeded to waste an entire hour of travel time with those basics. Jabeth and I, we listened, but after a while it got harder and harder to pay attention. Mr. Peece must have seen it, because he finally handed the weapon to Jabeth.

"Here you go, son. Do your worst."

Jabeth fondled the loaded weapon for a minute like it was holy. Then he raised it toward the tree. "See that little branch hanging out over the crick to the right?"

"What about it?" I asked.

Jabeth aimed and pulled the trigger. Just like that. The explosion near deafened me. After I finished blinking, that little branch wasn't there anymore.

"That's what." He handed the weapon to me, grinning. "Your turn, Simon."

I looked to Mr. Peece. He'd gone sort of pale all over. He swallowed. "Go ahead, Simon. Load her. Like Jabeth said, it's your turn."

I went through the entire procedure Mr. Peece had been explaining. Then I pointed to another branch and took my shot. The rifle barreled into my shoulder something fierce. I dropped the butt and rubbed at where it pained while opening my eyes hopefully. End result was, that cottonwood had no need to be scared of me.

"Anybody see where the shot went?"

Mr. Peece pointed about forty-five degrees across the prairie from the tree. "Somewheres over there."

"Oh."

He slapped me on the back. "Don't feel bad, Simon. We're not all born to be sharpshooters."

After that we let off another few rounds, then turned to head back to camp. Except we turned into unexpected company. There was a row of boys and men standing behind us—a half dozen of them. Must've crept up mighty quietly, out of complete nowhere. They was dressed in longish hair, leather pants, and ragged shirts almost worse than Jabeth's old duds. Their faces were dark, too, but not like Jabeth's. Closer to the fine bronze of my turkeys than chocolate. I opened my mouth and shut it. I tried again.

"Indians?"

"Looks like it, Simon," Mr. Peece said, real calm and collected. He lowered the rifle, now in his own left hand, and raised his right.

"How."

"Good morning," one of them answered. "Fine morning for shooting."

"Sure is." Mr. Peece's Adam's apple wobbled.

"Aside from the fact that you are currently on Indian reservation lands, where it is strictly illegal for any but tribal members to discharge weapons."

Mr. Peece's right hand dropped. "Well, now, I guess the boys and I ain't been careful enough about our geography. Whyn't you gentlemen head back to camp with us for a little breakfast and we can discuss our apologies over some beans and pan bread."

The Indian in charge nodded and we filed back through the grass.

It was lucky Mr. Peece had set the big cauldron to simmer with beans before we'd gone off for our lessons. Now he gave it a mighty stir and pulled out the frypan to start in on the hot bread. I broke into the corn and scattered some for the birds so's they wouldn't start marching down the trail in advance of us.

All this time our new acquaintances sort of poked around camp. Their leader was a man maybe about my pa's age—not quite as big, but looking to be hiding almost as much strength in the muscles beneath his faded blue shirt. Well, he started off admiring the horses. Then he and the others moved on to Sparky and his brothers. The younger Indians seemed real interested in the mules. Snowball even permitted a slim fellow to rub his ears, before trying for a nip at a tooth bracelet dangling from his wrist. Lastly, those Indians allowed themselves to comment on the existence of my turkeys. Meantime, Emmett kept a watchful eye on the lot of them. He wasn't real upset the way he'd been with my pa and Cleaver. More sort of on the alert, standing stiff on all four spindly, bowed legs.

Finally, we all hunkered down to the meal. I started in apologizing for the lack of proper plates, then shut my trap. The Indians were already solving the problem in the simplest way. They just took ahold of Mr. Peece's flat bread and scooped into the bean pot with it. We ate in silence till every bean and crumb of bread was gone. Three pots of coffee, too, passing the cups around. It was real communal.

The one in the faded blue shirt, who'd talked to us at the start, presently sank back on his haunches. I was kind of waiting for him to belch—or maybe let loose with a little gas—after consuming so many beans. But he didn't. Instead, he went and pulled out a handkerchief and dabbed at his mouth and fingers before tucking it away again. So much for wild Indians.

"Thank you for your hospitality."

His voice after all the quiet made me jump.

"You're probably wondering about us as much as we are about you and your unusual *herd*."

His lips parted over white teeth. "I am John Winter Prairie—the 'John' part courtesy of my teachers at Shawnee Mission as a boy." He motioned to his companions, all of them sprawled, comfortably digesting, but real alert nonetheless. Sort of like Emmett.

"We are Pottawattomie. Much diminished from our great days in the Wild Rice Country to the north, regrettably. But then, our grandfathers made a few bad business deals with your Great White Father in Washington. That—coupled with smallpox and an unfortunate taste for your whiskey . . ."

He paused, and I stole a fast look at Mr. Peece. My drover was nodding in complete understanding.

The Indian raised both palms. "Such things do tend to change one's future. What we've got left is a small area of this Kansas prairie. Very small. You can understand how we might wish to hold on to such as is remaining to us, however humble it may be. However insignificant our rules may seem to the passing world."

Jabeth had been making himself near-invisible, keeping very quiet, during the entire meal. Now he apparently couldn't hold his tongue another moment. "We didn't kill a single creature on your land, Mr. Winter Prairie, sir. Not even a rabbit. We was just in mind of a little target practice. For maybe catching us a buffalo up ahead. There's been rustlers after us, too, and—"

"Rustlers?" The Indian's dark eyes gave Jabeth a piercing look.

"Yes, sir. *Turkey* rustlers. After Simon here's entire worldly goods. Got the best of 'em once already back in Missouri, but they's like slave catchers in their

117

determination. Some folks just don't ever understand that certain things is private property. Like a man's soul"—Jabeth sat up straighter—"or these here lands of yours, which we didn't properly know was yours—"

"—but we'll be mighty pleased to vacate soon's we can hit the trail again," Mr. Peece finished.

"Paying you for any damage done, fair and square, though I don't rightly think there was any," I tacked on.

John Winter Prairie smiled at last. It softened the fierceness of his hawk-like nose. "You seem unusually honorable for men of the non-Indian persuasion."

He swung to his feet in one graceful movement. As if they'd been poised on springs, his friends followed suit. "Why don't we call your breakfast payment in full for any incursions unintentionally made." He studied us again and I could've swore I saw laughter in his eyes. "There's not much to do out here, after all, and we occasionally like to collect a little news of the world."

Mr. Peece wiped sweat from his face. "That's right neighborly of you gents. If you feel like another meal whilst we're still traversing your lands, feel free."

"Unfortunately, our lands do not extend much farther than another day's journey for you. We are compressed in a very tight box. And how much longer we have even this box is questionable."

"You mean you can't go beyond your lands?" I blurted out. "What if you need to hunt? For buffalo or something?"

"Don't look for buffalo on Pottawattomie lands—or anywhere else nearby. The great beast is long gone from here. The herds of millions are nearly no more."

I scratched my head. "How could that be? Millions of buffalo ought to last forever!"

"Ask your white hunters who kill them for sport, leaving their carcasses to rot!" The Indian visibly checked his anger. "But I think you aren't that sort of people."

"No, sir!"

"Uh-uh."

"No way."

We all shook our heads with force.

"I thought not. You seem reasonable." He surveyed the camp again. "Being reasonable men, you wouldn't care to trade for those two horses, would you?"

"Not on your life!" Mr. Peece blurted out. "I mean, I appreciate your interest in them, Mr. Winter Prairie, I surely do. But they's the start of my herd for farther out west. After we gets these turkeys to market in Denver."

John Winter Prairie nodded. "You have sound judgment in horseflesh. I wish you well in your travels."

Then they was gone, disappeared into the grass. The entire lot of Pottawattomie, without ever a peep from the rest of them. I turned to Mr. Peece.

"You sure they was Indians? I never heard nobody talk like that before. Not even the preacher at church.

119

And where was the feathers and moccasins and such? They wore boots same as you and me!"

Mr. Peece shook his head. "It's a frightening thing when even the Indians get civilized. A man don't know where he stands anymore. Still, Winter Prairie there was nice enough, even if he seemed to be doing a little jesting with us now and again."

He poked his nose into the bean pot. "Wasn't a thing strange about their appetites, though." His head bobbed up again. "Maybe we ought to consider standing watch the next few nights anyhow. Those Pottawattomie got themselves an inventory of our entire worldly goods."

❧ ELEVEN ❧

Nothing came during our night watch except the beginnings of a wind that was to whistle and moan and blow at us clear across the open prairie lands for days on end. That wind seemed to start just about where the last of the humans ended—Indians and settlers both. It wasn't till the next afternoon, though, that something else came out of the surrounding shoulder-high, bluestem grass that was seared brown and dry by the same wind.

First it was Jabeth, bolting from nowhere, a few partridges hanging from his belt. "Company coming!" he sang out in warning.

Mr. Peece stopped the wagon short. The horses, tied behind on loose ropes, danced to a halt. My birds started bunching into one another, their strides broken. Emmett ignored the birds and set into a barking jag. Bidwell Peece craned his neck and trained his eyes to the northeast, where even I could now see some sort of motion parting the tall grass.

"We're past the reservation already, ain't that so, Mr. Peece?" I asked with a sudden sense of foreboding.

"Got to be," he muttered. "Wonder what the rules truly is about Indians leaving their lands, versus white folks crossing them."

Jabeth was already by the rear of the wagon. "Want I should haul out the rifle, Mr. Peece, sir?"

"Rather you didn't. I got a distaste for violence in general. Also wouldn't do a whole pack of good if there's more of them than there is of us."

Jabeth didn't like that answer. "What we supposed to do, then? Just sit here a-waiting to be done in? Ain't a solitary place to take shelter on this blamed empty prairie. If there was some decent woods, at least . . ."

I clambered up the wagon next to Mr. Peece to get a better viewpoint. "Coming closer," I reported. "Seems to be only one batch, in a more or less straight line through the grass." I squinted some more, then let out a whistle. "Son of a gun!"

"What is it, Simon?" Mr. Peece stood on the bench next to me, and Jabeth clawed up the side, too.

"What in thunder!"

"Monsters!" Jabeth squeaked. "They's monsters comin' at us!"

I started to chuckle, then it grew into a belly laugh. Jabeth and Mr. Peece both pounded at me till I took control of myself again.

"Leggo! Stop!" I cried. "Ain't monsters at all, atall.

Nor Indians, neither. It's only camels—and they're carrying Pa and Cleaver!"

"That does it!" Jabeth scrambled down and headed for the wagon's rear. "Ain't nobody gonna stop me from loading the rifle this time!"

Pa and Cleaver must've gone back to their circus after all. Where else would they get camels—a whole family of them? For as they came closer, I couldn't help but recognize the papa camel that'd groaned so pitifully when loaded with burdens in the circus ring. Also the mama camel. Cleaver was riding her, just behind Pa. And behind them, loping to keep up, was the little fellow. Their gait was kind of unnatural, but maybe that's the way of it with camels. What also wasn't natural was what Pa and Cleaver was doing as they bore down on us.

"I don't believe it," Mr. Peece breathed out. "After all the water what's already flowed under the bridge. Even after mentioning them to the Indians, I never really believed—"

"That Pa and Cleaver would come after us again?"

"Right. And now those scoundrels are aiming rifles at us!"

Not only were they aiming, they were actually beginning to shoot.

"Duck!" I yelled, and acted accordingly.

Those shots shouldn't really have troubled me,

though. First off, they was aimed from the top of camels, which looked to be the closest thing to riding an earthquake I'd ever seen. And from what I understood, earthquakes wasn't conducive to straight shooting. Next, there was Jabeth, stretched out full length next to the wagon gate, ready to pick off anything that moved should he decide to pull his trigger. Why he didn't was a mystery. I snuck around the side of the wagon—the sheltered side—to find out exactly why.

"Why aren't you shooting back, Jabeth?" I stretched out next to him on the ground.

"They's still jerking around too much on them monsters. Wouldn't mind winging either of 'em a little, indeed I wouldn't." He kept his attention straight ahead at the oncoming enemy. "But I ain't got no heart for outright murder."

"Oh." I cogitated on that as Pa finally broke through the grass, camel complaining to high heaven. Beyond everything else, Pa was still my pa. "I guess I know what you mean. It's all right, Jabeth."

Cleaver broke through next. Finally came the little fellow. He stood there chuffing and staring at my wagon and mules and turkeys like *he'd* just come to the circus for the first time. My mules must've thought something similar, 'cause they started braying their blamed heads off.

So then we had what you might call a standoff. There was all the assorted livestock provoked with each other to high heaven. There was Emmett, barking himself hoarse. There was Pa and Cleaver pointing guns at us—and us pointing guns at them. At least, one gun. Pa spoke first. He had to raise his voice above the din to do so.

"Glad to see you still got your flock, Simon." He clutched at his mount a little queasily as it swayed beneath him. "Made good time, too."

"Considerate of you to worry over it all, Pa," I shouted back.

"He's just that kind of a fellow," piped up Cleaver from behind. "All the way clear from Russellville to Independence, where the circus boat was waiting, your pa just couldn't stop worrying over you and your birds, Simon. Wondering how far you were getting. Wondering if you were hanging on to those birds better than we did during our short period of acquaintance with them. In between peeling off patches of tar and turkey feathers, of course. The tarring and feathering was complimentary—thoughtfully performed by those Russellville folks you dumped us with."

"They was an interesting group of people," I opined.

Pa spit, then managed to nudge at his camel's middle. "Down, Ali!" He gave that order with more assurance in his voice than in his face, which seemed a mite on the green side.

It was fascinating watching what all a camel has to go through to get rid of its rider. All that groaning and tucking in of legs whilst first its front, then finally its rear hits the dirt. Not anywhere near as useful as a mule or horse that could easily be unmounted. With a final *whump*, Ali completed the process. Pa crawled off with evident relief, rifle foremost.

I was curious, so I figured it wouldn't hurt to ask a question. "How is it that you and Cleaver didn't make off with that other matched pair of Arabian horses at the circus, Pa? Instead of—"

"Instead of with these accursed dregs of the animal world?" Pa swung his free hand a little too close to Ali's mouth. The camel went for it, with a solid crunch of teeth.

"Ow!" Pa kicked at the camel and pulled his hand free. "Tarnation!" He nursed it under his armpit. "You see what I mean? You think we didn't go for those horses first?"

"Unfortunately," drawled Cleaver from his perch, "unfortunately, our old comrades had put a watch on the more valuable animals. As we really couldn't be expected to ride the lion or tiger, and as we had no interest in the trained dogs, our choice of transport was narrowed down."

Cleaver made sure that Pa was in control of his weapon again before kicking his own camel into a seated position. He removed himself with more aplomb than Pa had. "I've actually grown somewhat fond of Fatima here during our short closer acquaintance. Haven't I, Fatima?"

At that point, the little camel butted Cleaver out of the way to gain access to his mama.

"If it wasn't for this youngster that set up such a wail we had to bring him along . . ." Cleaver brushed himself down, then reached for his rifle again. "I'm afraid I find *all* children to be distasteful nuisances."

"Anyhow . . ." Pa got himself back into the conversation at last. He steadied wobbly legs, and burped, and his complexion turned healthier. "Anyhow, Cleaver and me put a lot of thought into what we done wrong with them birds the last time. We figure we're now in a position to improve our methods and get them safely to Denver. Seeing as how that's the case, we thought you all might consider a trade."

"A trade?" I asked. Folks sure had a high interest in trading these days.

"Yep. These here priceless camels straight from the mysterious East for your entire traveling establishment."

Mr. Peece let out a hoot behind me. I guessed that was a sort of hint, but I didn't need to think about Pa's suggestion for any length of time anyhow.

"Sorry, Pa. Camels is fine creatures, I'm sure. Specially on the far distant deserts of Egypt where they belongs. But I don't think the folks in Denver would want to pay me five thousand dollars for them, priceless or not—"

"Enough of this silly talk, Simon," Jabeth finally broke in. "Tell your pa and Cleaver that if they don't set down their weapons right fast, they's gonna be missing a few limbs."

Cleaver chuckled. "You have one gun. We have two. What happens after you use your shot? Think there'll be time to reload?"

"You didn't have time to reload your guns, either," Jabeth pointed out—reasonably, I thought.

"Ah, but we have *two* rifles each."

Without turning, Cleaver motioned behind to his camel. Sure enough, another rifle was slung from her hump. Hadn't noticed it in the rush of events.

"These rifles in hand"—Cleaver gestured—"these are fully loaded. I don't lie. This is no coconut shy."

I looked to Mr. Peece, who hadn't said aught the entire time, discounting his hoot. He only squatted there, holding back Emmett, trying to keep the little dog from taking on both Pa and Cleaver single-handed. I saw my drover's shoulders slump in defeat.

What now? I wondered. Was we all just going to lounge around here under the hot sun and dry winds listening to my mules bray and my turkeys gobble till kingdom come? I guess I forgot about Jabeth again, even though he was sprawled out right next to me. But he must've noticed Mr. Peece's dejection, too. Only, he decided on action.

"I ain't giving up so easy." He raised the barrel of his rifle and let loose. In a moment, Cleaver's right hand dropped its weapon, and his left snatched for the wounded arm. Pa hesitated with his firearm a second too long. Maybe he was figuring on whether he truly wanted to shoot his only son, too. I'd like to think that was the case. Meanwhile, other things was beginning to happen, but it took a while to figure them all out.

Something else swept out of the grass surrounding us. A bunch of somethings, bare-chested and done up with war paint. Swinging rifles and hatchets and whooping up a storm. My mouth dropped open as I realized these was *Indians*! True, blood-and-thunder Indians! I didn't know where to look anymore. At Pa and Cleaver? At my fine turkeys, under attack from all sides?

Jabeth paid no attention, only started in reloading his gun fast as he could. It still takes time, though, and when he was finally ready to aim again, that whole situation was already over.

I crawled up from my spot in the dirt. I blinked, feeling in a daze. Pa and Cleaver was being bound hand and foot by men who suddenly looked a lot like our Pottawattomie under all that amazing war paint. I walked closer.

"Mr. Winter Prairie?" I asked, searching through the stripes of red and yellow on his high-boned cheeks. "Is that you underneath all that?"

He grinned. "It would seem to be."

"But I thought you Pottawattomie was peace-loving hunters and farmers."

"We are." He checked to make certain his friends

was doing a solid job with those ropes. "But occasionally we get bored. We also get curious when strangers on *camels* cross our reservation—without a by-your-leave. We begin to put two and two together. As the official peacekeepers for our territory, we feel it incumbent upon ourselves to see that nothing unorthodox occurs on our lands."

"But . . ." I tried. "But, sure and certain, we're way past your lands by this time—"

"That would be a matter of interpretation of boundaries, would it not? And all white men know that Indians are too uneducated to truly perceive such concepts as *boundaries.*"

"But—" My head was truly reeling by this time.

"But nothing, Simon." Mr. Peece was by my side at last. He stretched out his fingers to Mr. Winter Prairie. "May I have the honor of shaking your hand, sir? Never saw such perfect timing in my life."

They shook.

Mr. Peece gave me a nudge and I shook, too. Finally, Jabeth completed the process. All this time the camels was staring at us like we was out of our minds. The turkeys, too. A thought came to me.

"Mr. Winter Prairie?"

He listened.

"Sir. I'd like to thank you for your help. You and all your friends." I pointed at some of his younger comrades, who was currently having a good roaring laugh

130

over Pa and Cleaver trussed up in the middle of the road. "I'd like to make you a present, too. You surely deserve it. Ain't like a payment or anything"—I'd remembered almost insulting Jabeth some time back—"just a freewill gift from me to you and your entire tribe. Something of your liking."

John Winter Prairie's eyes immediately shot to Mr. Peece's prize Arabians. Then they noted the look on the older man's face. The Indian turned his attention to my other livestock.

"I thank you for your kind offer. And I must admit I've been thinking about turkeys, young man, since we last met. Historically, some of my people considered them stupid and cowardly—"

My mouth opened in protest, but Mr. Winter Prairie just pressed on.

"—and they refused to eat them for fear of acquiring those characteristics." He paused to study my flock. "A shortsighted attitude, I'm afraid." A shrug. "But your birds exhibit something grander . . . and it's time for us to move into the modern age, as far as poultry husbandry is concerned. We still have a few wild turkeys locally, but if that stock were to be mixed with a little fresh blood . . ."

I gulped. "Yes, sir. That'd be a fine idea. How many would you like?"

"How many hens will a tom mate with in the spring?"

Knowing a fair amount about such things, I blurted it out before considering. "Ten to twelve hens to the tom, sir. The hens'll lay you thirty to forty eggs each by late March. A few seasons of that, and you've got yourself a flock of your own."

He nodded gravely, then pulled out the handkerchief I recalled and began to scrub at his face paint. "Curious stuff, this. I'm not even certain we got the old patterns right. No one seems to remember, exactly. But bold colors did seem to be called for." He finished the scrubbing. "How about a dozen hens, then? And two toms. Just to be safe. Throw in the camels if you don't know what to do with them. We might try breeding them, as well."

I breathed a sigh of relief. It could've been worse. Much worse. And I'd already begun wondering what to do with the camel critters, seeing as how my mules appeared to take offense over them. "You've got a deal, sir." I paused. "If you'll promise to keep my pa and Cleaver, too."

Mr. Winter Prairie's attention shot to the captives. "That giant's your father?"

I nodded sadly. "I guess we never quite took as family. Don't hurt him, please. But I'd sooner get to Denver on my own."

He studied Pa again. "I can understand that. Excessive punishment shouldn't be necessary." Winter Prairie's glance passed my pa to focus on the flock. "My choice?"

"Yes, sir. They's all fine, solid birds."

Well, I guess it hurt a little to see another fourteen of my flock disappearing. But it was for a good cause. It was nice thinking my turkeys might be the start of something useful for these peaceful-type Pottawattomie. In a few years, they could be walking birds to Denver themselves.

It didn't pain that much to say goodbye to my pa again, though. He shot me a look that could kill before commencing to make noises worse than the camels when they all slunk off through the tall grass. Cleaver didn't say boo. He was too busy wincing over his wounded arm that Jabeth had solicitously wrapped up for him.

"It was a nice clean shot, Mr. Cleaver," Jabeth said as he did the work. "The ball went clear through your upper muscle and out again, just like I planned. It shouldn't be much more than a little sore for a while if you keep it tended."

After they'd all disappeared, Mr. Peece went around inspecting things. "Looks to be a little late in the day to set off again, Simon. Any problems with just bedding down on the spot?"

I shook my head no.

Mr. Peece bent to pick up one discarded rifle, then another. "We seem to be collecting us an entire armory, boys. Sure hope it don't portend things to come."

ᘔ TWELVE ᘔ

There did turn out to be some folks past the Pottawattomie. We never could be sure of exactly who or what to expect, though. This was because we was journeying now through what Mr. Peece called virgin land—on account of he never personally been over the terrain in his earlier travels. But it didn't make me worried about getting lost, because no matter what, we still had to follow water. The birds and four-legged creatures would always need plenty to drink at the end of each day. And Mr. Peece said that if we kept following the Kansas River like we was at the present time, and the Smoky Hill Fork when it branched off, why then, sooner or later, we'd get us into the foothills near to Denver.

Still, it was a little surprising when the first people we came across was cavalry soldiers from Fort Riley. That was only a couple of days past seeing the last of my pa and Cleaver. The thought did strike me in passing—before we met up with the real article—that it might've been considerably easier on my finances if the U.S. Cavalry had come to the rescue instead of Mr. John Winter Prairie and his Pottawattomie. Then I studied my birds again and decided not to be greedy. If those Indians hadn't been as honest as they was, *they* could've had my entire establishment a sight easier than Pa. As it stood now, I'd just sort of spread a little friendship and turkey culture, same as that Johnny Appleseed that Miss Rogers used to tell us about in school.

So I started thinking about Miss Rogers again. Wouldn't she be pleased we'd gotten as far as we had! It was hard to believe she didn't even know about Jabeth, or my meeting up with Pa and Cleaver, or the Indians. She'd enjoy those stories fine.

I was walking along my turkeys' right flank, making up a letter in my head trying to explain all of it to Miss Rogers, and wondering how I'd ever get it all down on real paper. Every time I put a quill pen or pencil stub between my thick fingers, the letters just sort of came out backwards or upside down, no matter how hard I tried. I guess my brain must've been practically back in Union, Missouri, worrying out the letter business instead of paying attention right here in the Kansas Territory, 'cause when that first shot rang out, I near to jumped from my skin.

Only then did I hear the horses bearing down, and the whoops.

"*Whooee!* I got me one!"

"Dang. Missed."

My eyes opened wide and my head cleared itself right fast. It was mounted blue-coated soldiers, surrounding us on all sides. Seemed near to a regiment of them. And they was taking potshots at my turkeys!

"Hey! What'd you think you're doing? Stop!"

I stumbled over a body and stooped to pick up a hen gasping her last gasp. "There now," I whispered to her, smoothing the beautiful feathers. "There now. Guess you'll never get to see Denver."

I ran up to the rear of the wagon, which Mr. Peece'd stopped, and laid the hen gently atop a mountain of corn. Turkey heaven, for sure. As I wiped my bloodied hands on my trousers I felt another righteous anger grow in me, worse than that time with Cleaver and his coconut tricks. I spun around to the soldiers grinning at my nervous flock from atop their horses. Their rifles was already pointed and ready to shoot another round.

"I'll—I'll personally thrash any man so much as sets his finger to a trigger again," I managed to splutter out. It was hard, on account of I was burning hot all over, and could even feel my heart pumping. "What right have you to go after my birds? I thought soldiers was supposed to protect innocent civilians!"

"Out of the way, boy," one soldier yelled. "We ain't had nothin' to shoot at in too long."

"Injuns is almost gone," said another, "and there

ain't no wild game left fifty miles to either side of the fort." He sighted down his gun barrel.

That was provocation enough for me. I stomped off toward him and his horse, fire in my eyes.

"Take it easy, Simon," Mr. Peece urged from atop the wagon.

"Beyond taking it easy I am."

In another moment I was hauling that soldier right out of his saddle, toppling him into the dust where he belonged. The rest of the cavalry, I guess they could've shot me right then and there, but their sporting instincts seemed to get the better of them. Weapons was lowered as they nudged their horses into a circle around the dismounted soldier and me.

"Come on, Clancy," one fellow egged him on. "Give this farmer boy what for!"

Clancy struggled to his feet, brushed down his uniform, and squared off into a boxing stance I'd once seen some fellows use outside the saloon in Union. I raised my fists in imitation.

"Swing at 'im, Clancy!"

"Give him your left hook!"

Clancy swung. But since his friends had already told me about his left hook, I was already ducking. I stood for another couple of swings after that, just swaying to one side or the other out of range of his fists, then decided boxing was a silly way to try to win a fight. I bunched up my own right fist as if I was going to go for this Clancy's broad red face. Instead,

I lowered my head just like Uncle Lucas's bull back home and rammed at his barrel chest.

"*Oomph!*"

The wind went out of that soldier right fast, I can tell you. I stood over his body a long minute. Then I looked up at the others. "Which one of you turkey-murdering villains is next?"

One of them was already easing off his mount, and I would've took him easy, too, if another soldier hadn't come riding up. There was gold braid all over his shoulders, and his campaign hat, too. This one must be an officer.

"Atten-*shun!*"

Never saw anybody put in order as fast as them soldiers. In a minute even their horses was lined up in a straight row.

"Sergeant Johnson!"

"Captain Masters, sir!" the soldier now at the head of the row barked back.

"Explain exactly what is happening here, sergeant!"

"Sir." The sergeant looked flustered. "Sir, we was just having us a little fun."

"Fun?" I roared, the anger still in me. "They was using my turkey flock for target practice, is what they was doing. Just out of the blue they comes swooping down, shooting their guns off. And us totally unarmed and innocent! Killed at least one of my birds, and upset the rest out of a month's growth, too!"

The captain turned his steely eyes back to the sergeant. "Is this the truth, Johnson?"

"*I'll* tell you it's the honest truth," Mr. Peece joined in from atop his wagon seat. "We've survived Indians and rustlers already, and I'd take on any of 'em again sooner than your *cavalry* here." Mr. Peece said that word *cavalry* like it was a dirty one.

The captain just sat straight as an arrow astride his big chestnut horse, eyeing his men on the edge of the prairie to one side, us in the middle of the rutted trail, and the soldier I'd bested decorating the dust between. "What happened to Trooper Clancy?"

"He was aiming to shoot at my birds again," I answered. "I fought him fair and square. And I won. I'll take on the whole, entire U.S. Army if I have to. Nobody attacks me and mine without cause."

"Admirably put, young man," that captain said. "We could use a few good men like you in this man's army. Ever think of enlisting?"

"No, sir. And after today, don't suppose I ever will, either."

The captain considered that for a long moment. Then he turned to the sergeant. "Johnson. You and your platoon are on report. Sling Clancy over his saddle and return to camp."

I watched the sergeant's face turn hard and cold as the captain addressed me again.

"What's your name, young man?"

"Simon, sir. Simon Green."

"I'll make a note of that. You may put in a request for reimbursement of any valuables lost in this unauthorized skirmish. Send it to the Superintendent of the Army in Washington City. Cite the location—just east of Fort Riley in the Kansas Territory—and the date. I shall make a suitable report myself."

"Yes, sir."

I said that as if I was truly going to do it. But the point was beyond me. I didn't figure I'd live to see the day the government way back in Washington City was about to pay up, Denver price, for a few birds shot by its rowdy troops. Not if they was putting all their energy into harassing civilians and chasing Indians off their lands.

"Yes, sir. I just might do that."

"Excellent," Captain Johnson replied. "Always work through the proper channels. Only way to get things done." He tipped his hat to Mr. Peece, then to me. "I wish you an uneventful continuation of your journey, wherever it may be taking you."

The captain pulled at his reins and was gone, trotting his mount across the grassy prairie due north-northwest.

Mr. Peece waited till the whole lot of them was way beyond hearing range. Then he tore off his hat and flung it at the ground. "Byoo-reaucracy!" he spat. "Glad I'm heading farther West. Hope to get so far

140

West I won't never have to hear about government no more."

Jabeth's head suddenly poked out of a patch of dried grass. "Is they gone? All gone?"

I spun on him. "Where've *you* been, Jabeth? Could've used some moral support here, I surely could've."

"Sorry, Simon." He hung his head for the first time in days. "But the Missouri militia—the pro-slavery one? My old master used to belong to it. Can't say I ever took to soldiers. No."

I swung between Jabeth, Mr. Peece still on the wagon, and my flock. Them toms was gobbling up a storm. The hens, who never did do any gobbling, were clicking to beat the band. They was all going around in circles, heads bobbing, flustered as bad as when my pa was in charge of them. "We have to calm these birds. Think a corn supper would help?"

Mr. Peece finally eased off the wagon and stretched his back. "Wouldn't hurt. They're too wound up for any more traveling today, that's for certain. How many did we lose?"

"Only the one for sure. But I haven't looked real close. I hate to do it, but I think we're having turkey for supper."

Mr. Peece bent to comfort Emmett, who'd been whining by the rear of the wagon where I'd set the shot bird. "Come on, Emmett," I overheard him mur-

141

mur. "Ain't all humans as thoughtless as the ones we been mostly meeting up with lately. Let's you and me see to the mules and horses."

I broke out the corn and Jabeth started in cleaning my lost hen. She cooked up more tender than I'd expected after all the miles of muscle-stretching she'd done walking from Missouri. And there was a lot of her—all bittersweet from her useless sacrifice.

We saw Fort Riley off in the distance the next morning. It was a bunch of buildings clustered to the north side of the Kansas River. None of us had any desire to inspect the Army camp at closer quarters. We swung around past, then came to where the Smoky Hill Fork flowed into the bigger Kansas. It was a relief to get that last piece of civilization behind us. Far as I was concerned, I didn't care if we never saw another two-legged critter till we found Denver.

✎ THIRTEEN ✎

That Smoky Hill Fork went into a series of watery twists and bends that kept us busy for nearly a week till it unraveled itself some. By the time we got to the straighter part, we was in true wilderness country, with the trail mostly disappeared. It was nothing but mile after mile of hot sun baking us, baking the tall grass that flowed like an ocean under the prairie winds. Not that *I* knew what an ocean looked like, but Mr. Peece claimed he'd been born near one.

"Yep. Spent my baby days by the Atlantic," he remarked late one afternoon as I walked alongside the wagon, just about ready to call it a day. "Waves would flow in and out in patterns like to this here grass. It was in the south of New Jersey. Once you got past the ocean and the marshes, the land was flat, too. A lot like this. But you couldn't see forever, the way you can here."

"Forever? Never thought about it thataways." I squinted past the westering sun. That's when I spotted the little humpy rise just ahead. Something growing out of the prairie sod. Also noticed some dark storm clouds forming dead ahead.

"Think we'll get any rain tonight?"

Bidwell Peece swiped at his brow. "It'd be due. Long overdue. But the air don't have a rainy sort of feel to it."

I swiped at my own face, though I didn't need to. Things was so bone-dry the sweat had been all leeched out of me. I was being tanned stiff as leather. I turned back to my birds, and we closed in the quarter mile to that odd rise.

Would've moved right on beyond it, if it hadn't turned into a soddy—one of them little dugout houses built halfway into the earth from squares of sod turf. Might've still moved beyond, thinking it deserted, if a wild figure hadn't of come bolting out of it, screeching like a banshee. Thin arms was flailing, legs churning, skirts blowing in the wind.

Skirts? Could this raging thing be a woman? I stopped cold.

"Mercy!" she cried. "Have mercy on me! Save me from this godforsaken place!"

All the rest of us stopped, too, including the birds, on account of she'd flung herself down, smack in front of the wagon. Mr. Peece couldn't do other than haul up real hard on Sparky and the other mules.

"Whoa! Whoa, now!" He stared at her as she lay mere inches from the heaving animals' hooves.

I loped up front and stared with him. The poor creature was a sight, with her long hair undone and askew, her skirts in shreds, and prairie dust coating every inch of her.

"Ma'am?" I reached down to raise her up, but she only sprawled, near-lifeless in my arms. I looked closer. She weren't actually a ma'am. More of a miss. Underneath the gray dust and sunken cheeks was a young lady.

"Miss?"

Her limp figure jerked, her eyes opening and closing in spasms. "Save me," she whispered. "Save me from this desolation of body and soul!"

I glanced up to Mr. Peece. He was shaking his head sorrowfully. "Prairie madness. I heard tell of it. From being out here with nothin' but the winds to listen to. Probably a touch of the ague, besides, from the looks of her."

I stood there, sheltering the poor little thing in my arms. "What'll I do with her?"

Mr. Peece creaked off the wagon seat. "I guess we've made most of our miles for the day, though I was hoping to get closer to the next bend of the fork, shallow though it be. Seem to have lost sight of the water for the moment." He studied me and my burden again. "Try taking her into the house. Ought to be a bed you can set her onto."

I looked back at him, frightened. "You want me to tend to her all by myself?"

"You're a big fellow, Simon. Ought to be able to handle the job. It ain't like she's got the energy to bite you." He cracked a smile. "Somebody's got to see to the animals and get supper going."

Jabeth turned up about then. "We stopping? Got nothin' but one scrawny rabbit. Those soldiers was lying about only having done in all the game in fifty miles—" He noticed the girl at last. His mouth gaped open. "Whatcha got there, Simon?"

"What does it look like?" I felt suddenly foolish planted in the middle of the overgrown trail with my drooping burden. "Why don't you give Mr. Peece a hand ungearing the mules so he can start up a little rabbit broth for this here young lady?"

Jabeth's jaw clicked shut, then opened again. "Sure thing, Simon. But what about water for the birds? They's looking thirstier than usual, and—"

A shrill screech from the bundle in my arms near blasted out my eardrums.

"The wrath of God! The wrath of God is upon us!" A trembling arm was pointing toward the sky.

My head bobbed up. Sure enough, that black storm cloud was closing in on us. "Ain't nothing but some rain coming, miss. Seems to me you could use a little rain—"

"Noooo!" she wailed. "They wouldn't let me go. Held on to me, every one of them. Pulled at me from the very earth—"

146

I shook my head at Mr. Peece. He nodded know-ingly. She kept on ranting.

"The Lord said to let His people go, but they wouldn't! I'm one of His people. I am! Tell me I am!"

"Sure and certain—" I tried, but she wasn't listening.

"He gave a warning! 'I will bring the locusts into thy coast: And they shall cover the face of the earth, that one cannot be able to see the earth . . . And they shall fill thy houses, and the houses of all thy servants, and the houses of all the Egyptians . . .' "

"Egyptians?" My eyes shot back to Mr. Peece. "I don't rightly understand—"

"She's quotin' from the book of Exodus," Jabeth broke in. "From the Bible. I knows that piece fine on account of it were all about escapin' from bondage. The plague of locusts, that come after the hail didn't work, and just afore the destruction of every single firstborn child—"

Another screech broke Jabeth's recitation. We all followed the crazy girl's shaking hand as her fingers pointed yet again.

"Maybe she ain't so crazy," I allowed after I'd seen what she was seeing. "Those there storm clouds ain't made of water no matter how you look at it. Water clouds never buzzed. They's made up of—"

"Grasshoppers!"

It was Jabeth screeching now, beginning to slap all over his body like he'd gone insane, too. In a split second I'd dropped my burden and was slapping, myself. That cloud had fallen all over us, and it was filled with grasshoppers! Hundreds, thousands, millions of them, landing on everything in sight. And their jaws was grinding, ready to chew into anything they could find. Anything at all.

The mules let out tortured brays. I tried to keep my eyes open long enough to check my birds. Was this to be the end of them, the end of us all?

"Son of a gun!"

Had to clap my hand over my mouth after I'd let that out. Nearly got a mouthful of the biggest, ugliest bugs I'd ever laid eyes on. But a chuckle almost forced my mouth open again. My turkeys wasn't being attacked. Far from it. They was snapping at those insects as if they'd never seen anything as delectable in their entire lives. Right and left they went at 'em, pecking, swallowing, pecking again, like they'd never get their fill.

I picked up the girl once more and hauled her into the center of the flock. Mr. Peece and Jabeth caught on and followed. We just sat ourselves down there, covered our heads, and waited for my turkeys to save the day.

It was twilight by the time the steady droning of grinding grasshopper jaws stopped. It was the stillness, the awesome sudden silence, that made me pull away my shielding arms and open my eyes. Somehow that young lady had ended up with her head in my lap. I'd been protecting her the entire time, sort of half-aware of the situation, while the plaguey hordes was surrounding us. I let out a whistle and Jabeth and Mr. Peece came out of their cocoons, too. Even Emmett lifted the front paws he'd flung over his eyes.

"I'll be . . ." Mr. Peece started.

"Look at them birds!" Jabeth's voice was filled with wonder. "I knew all along, every minute, there was a good reason to love turkeys!"

I felt like a proud papa as I surveyed my bloated flock. They was wobbling around worse than when we pulled off the water-drinking contest. Only this time it was almost a thousand nearly bursting birds stumbling around blissfully. If turkeys could belch, we would've been blown straight back to Missouri, wagon and all.

I hunted for the grasshoppers. All that was left in sight was neat little piles of thin black legs. Must be the least tasty part of a 'hopper.

"Don't think the birds'll be needing the river tonight," I commented unnecessarily as we all watched them begin scratching together sleeping nests in the dry grass. "Wouldn't be room in them for the water."

Mr. Peece struggled to his feet. "Still need to get some water into the mules and horses. But it's getting dark fast."

I felt a motion in my lap. Looking down, I remembered the girl and watched as her eyes fluttered open.

"The well," she whispered. "Water in the well behind the house. Not enough for the lost corn . . . Enough for you."

Mr. Peece stared down at her. "Looks like this is where I get to use that copper washtub again. Should suit our four-legged friends just fine as a watering trough."

The girl's lids drooped shut again. I collected her in my arms and finally headed into that house of hers. Once inside, I wished I hadn't. First off, I had to hunch down almost in half to squint through the darkness. She had some kind of a dim, earthy-smelling fire burning off in one corner. Aside from that, the only other things in the tiny room was a cobbled-together table and bench and one squat bed. I set her atop the bed gently, pulled up a quilt against the growing cool of the night winds, and scuttled from the gloom. Mr. Peece was standing out back.

"Find the well?"

"Not yet, Simon. Found something else, though." He motioned toward a row of low mounds with little stick crosses spiking out of them. I moved closer and frowned at the writing cut into the wood. There was barely enough light to work it all out.

Father, one said. *Mother*, read another. Then there was the little ones: *Brother Tom, Brother John, Sister Sarah, Baby Ada.*

I scratched my head. "Seems like more than a plague of locusts come through this place. Seems like the poor thing got a reason for her prairie madness."

Mr. Peece raised an arm around my shoulder. "It do seem that way, son."

We stood there for a while until we noticed the mules complaining out front. Mr. Peece let his arm drop. "Guess I better find that well."

I turned from the graves. "Guess I better see about the young lady. Maybe put the cookpot onto the little fire she's got inside."

I sat next to her bed all night. Couldn't sleep. I just propped myself against the wall with my blanket around my shoulders, listening to the wind tearing around the sod house. Listening to mice and other creatures scrambling across the dirt floor and up the dirt walls. Breathing in the dankness that held on to the place despite the hard drought outside. Hearing the soft, steady breathing of the little thing that'd swallowed the rabbit broth we fed her, then collapsed again as if she hadn't slept for a year.

I never could've rested here, anyways, surrounded by the wind and the ghosts of those graves outside. I wondered how her entire family had been done in. Wondered why they'd come to this place of desolation to begin with. Wondered how we could leave her in the morning.

I finally rubbed my eyes as the first dim shafts of dawn broke through cracks in the sod. That's when I knew we couldn't do it. Couldn't leave her here.

I felt better then, and turned to touch her arm.

"You stayed with me all night."

I started at her whisper. "You're awake?"

"Yes. For a long time. Thank you. You saved me. One more day would have been the end. I knew it. If the Lord hadn't taken me, I'd have taken myself."

It made me shiver to hear her talk such talk. "Hush. Ain't no way to speak. No way to be thinking." I needed to get away from that subject. "What's your name?"

"Lizzie. Elizabeth Hardwick. Last of the family. Last of the Hardwicks. They all . . . every one of them—"

I put a finger on her lips. "Be still, now. I know. I'm Simon. Simon Green. You can come with us, come with me. Far as you need to go."

"You're the biggest angel I've ever imagined." Her eyes drifted closed again. "Coming out of the wind . . . slaying the plague of locusts . . . so huge and strong . . ."

I bumbled up at her words and struck my head on the low roof of the dugout. Hard. I rubbed where it hurt. Me? An angel? That was a good one. I stumbled from the dark, dank room into the fresh, clean morning air.

Mr. Peece was already up, watering the mules again.

"I think we got us another mouth to feed, Mr. Peece."

He gave Snowball a loving stroke. "Figured as much. Get the coffee working, Simon. On the fire I got going out here."

I felt like giving that little man a hug. I gave it to one of the mules instead. "Right away, Mr. Peece. Right away."

❡ FOURTEEN ❡

No. *Please*. Just let me leave in peace!"

Lizzie Hardwick would've walked away from that dugout with nothing if I hadn't of gone in and rooted around myself. I came out with a carpet-bag I'd stuffed with the clothes I could find, a little stoneware bowl and spoon, and the quilt from last night, because I knew we was short on extra blankets. I brought out something else, too, but that I stowed in the wagon amongst the corn till she could face it better.

Jabeth and I propped her up on the wagon seat next to Mr. Peece and started moving the birds. They was a little on the slow side this morning. I guess they was still glutted from their grasshopper feast. But we all brightened after we'd gone a few miles and couldn't see that soddy left behind to sink back into the earth.

By the time we came to camp down that afternoon, Lizzie was acting considerable stronger. Jabeth and me took her down to the Smoky Hill Fork, and we all had a good bath to soak off the prairie dust and the feelings that'd been strong with us. Not all together, or in the altogether, of course. After Jabeth and I had splashed around some, Lizzie grabbed our lump of soap and chased us two back to camp. When she turned up later, I couldn't believe it was the same person.

She was still thin, still tattered, but you could see the color of her hair now. Her eyes, too. Her hair was a sort of shining dark bay, with glints of red in it from the setting sun. It fell thick and full all the way to her waist. And her eyes was a bright blue—like the ocean, I guessed right off. Also, she was smiling. At me.

She handed back the slick soap. "Thank you, Simon. For stopping to care for me when you had all your turkeys to worry about." She gazed around at the flock settling into their nesting places for the night. "Your amazing turkeys, that you walked so far from their home. Thank you for everything. Again."

I hardly caught her words, I was so floored by the whole effect of that soap. She'd turned out right nice. A perfect little lady. She even talked like Miss Rogers, though she couldn't be no older than Jabeth and me.

"Ain't noth—noth—" I stammered to a stop, then tried again. "Nothin' to thank me for, Miss Lizzie."

"*Lizzie* is just fine all by itself, Simon."

"Right, Miss Liz—I mean—"

Jabeth walked right in on the moment. "You don't know what you mean, Simon, you're that tongue-tied."

He grinned at Lizzie. "Now that we got you, we got to figure out your talent, girl. Everybody here's got to have a talent. Got to contribute to Simon's enterprise."

"Hush up, Jabeth!"

He turned on me. "Just 'cause she's female makes her different? That don't seem fair to me, Simon, no matter how you looks at it."

"No, it's not that atall. It's just that she's got to . . ." I stalled, trying to come up with a reason. I was real pleased when one popped into my head. "She's got to have a little time to *ac-climate*."

"You didn't give me no time to ac-climate! She's got to pitch right in—"

"Stop talking about me as if I weren't standing right here. Both of you!" Lizzie Hardwick flashed those blue eyes at both of us. "You think I'm still half out of my mind, don't you!"

"Well, you was a little, a little *unusual* yesterday," Jabeth tried.

"And wouldn't you be, too, if you'd had to bury your entire family single-handed? Baby Ada, she hung on to the very end. Kept me going in my need to care for her—" Lizzie's face squinched up, close to tears.

"You don't have to explain all that," I threw in fast. "None of it. I knows it was a trial for you—"

"No." Those blue eyes unsquinched and stormed steel gray just like that. "You don't. You'll never know exactly how bad it was. No one could. Yesterday morning when I patted down the last bit of earth over Baby Ada, when I threw away the shovel . . . I just *knew* it was the worst moment of my sixteen years on this earth. I just *knew* nothing worse could happen, but nothing better, either. There wasn't anything left. Nothing but a great, gaping void . . ."

I stopped paying much attention after she spilled out that figure about her age. *Sixteen.* My heart kind of dropped into its own void, whatever that was. A mighty evocative word, anyhow. She was *sixteen.* An older woman. No older woman would take a second glance at fifteen-year-old Simon Green, angel or not. Hopes dashed, I spun on my heels, leaving Jabeth to finish the commiserations.

I was down by the water, giving Sparky a bath with a vengeance, when Mr. Peece walked up.

"Thought I was in charge of the four-legged live-stock, Simon."

"You are," I grunted.

"Then why you rubbing off half of Sparky here's growth of coat with lye soap that don't agree with mules nohow?"

"Huh?" The cake of lye slipped through my fingers. It gave me an excuse to bend down into the knee-deep water to grasp for it. When I straightened up again, Mr. Peece was already dumping a bucket of water over my efforts. There did seem to be a noticeable bald patch where I'd been scrubbing for what must've been longer than I remembered. "Oh."

"Oh?" Mr. Peece echoed. He eyed me again, then scooped more water over Sparky. "If you feel a need to let out some aggravations, son, try not to do it on the livestock. You still got that much energy left after a full day's journey, take yourself off into the tall grass and try to find somethin' burnable. Ain't been a tree for a hundred miles, and we're gonna have to be tearin' the wagon apart for fuel soon, you expect any hot meals."

"Oh." I hadn't been thinking of meals at all. Not of Sparky, either, while I was busy giving him that bald spot. Only thing in my head had been Lizzie Hardwick. Sixteen-year-old Lizzie Hardwick. How, even scrawny as she currently was, she had the makings of true elegance. How she stood up to Jabeth and me so ladylike when she lost her temper the way she did. How she was gonna be pure catnip for all them bachelor miners that must be roaming around a gold town like Denver, just a-waitin' on our turkey dinners.

"Simon?"

I jumped. "What, Mr. Peece?"

"You got something on your mind, son?"

I shook my head vehemently. "No, sir. Not me. Nothing at all, atall on Simple Simon's mind. Never was, never could be."

"Son—" He stopped splashing at Sparky and

frowned. "Son, the birds and the bees ain't a pretty subject. Leastways, not at your age. You want to be careful—"

"Ain't nothing to be careful about, Mr. Peece. Ain't nobody to notice me, nohow."

I turned and stalked off again. Why should anybody notice me? Why should anyone of the female persuasion notice a hulking, stumbling, tongue-tied, overgrown boy? I shoved my way into the grass to find something to burn just a little bit hotter than I was already feeling.

The next week of travel was a hard one. This time it had nothing to do with new humans, of which we came across nary a one. It had nothing to do with the trail, which was working itself through a scabby sort of half prairie, half sagebrush desert. It had nothing to do with my birds, either. They was doing just fine. When it seemed like they wasn't finding enough nourishment between the sage and leftover drought-stricken grass, we broke out the corn again, and that kept them hale and hearty. Fact is, we broke out so much that the grain level in the bed of the wagon began noticeably lowering itself. Of course, that made my mules' work easier, so they was happy, too. It also brought to light a few surprises.

"Mr. Peece?" I called out late one afternoon after unloading the flock's meal.

"Yes, Simon?" He came trotting over.

"You know anything about these here implements that's beginning to stick out of the corn load everywheres?"

Mr. Peece, he took on an embarrassed look. "Well, son . . ."

"Well, what? You knew I didn't have no money to buy farming gear when we left Missouri. So where'd this plow come from?" I jabbed at the iron prong emerging from the mound of kernels. "When I jumped in the wagon bed after the corn"—I rubbed at my rear quarters and gave him an accusing look—"Near to give me a serious injury where I least expected it."

Bidwell Peece ran calloused fingers across his mouth. Didn't know better, I'd think he was hiding a smirk.

"So?" I pushed him. "Anything else in there I should know about? For my protection?"

"Simon, Simon." Mr. Peece shook his head. "It's just that you sees most things in this life in sheer black and white—"

"What's that supposed to mean?" I barked. The whole subject was beginning to make me tetchy. And I'd been tetchy enough the livelong week.

"You being so taken with Lizzie and all—"

"I ain't noways taken with Lizzie!" I bellowed. Then I lowered my voice and gave a quick look around to make sure she wasn't in hearing distance. "Just asked you a simple, civil question. I'd favor an answer in the same fashion."

"Simon"—he put out a hand to touch my arm—"Simon, all them people back at that soddy was *dead*. They didn't need farming implements where they lay. We *do*. To set up a new life out by Denver or beyond. And such implements might be hard to come by in mining country."

"You mean to say—"

"I mean I just borrowed what the Lord left there for our taking. Some extra harness and saddles, a few tools—"

"But they belong to Lizzie! And she didn't want them touched. Nohow, noways!"

He patted my arm. "They'll still belong to Lizzie farther west, Simon. Think of them as a kind of dowry—"

"For some plug-ugly, bearded man old enough to be her pa?" I yelled. I dove at the plow. Had every intention of lugging it out and tossing it into the sagebrush. Let the vultures and coyotes and wolves we'd started in hearing and seeing deal with it. Let it turn to solid rust and crumble when the rains finally bit into the drought.

"What're you two going on about?" Jabeth sauntered over. "Never heard you fighting before."

"Ain't fighting!" I roared.

Jabeth staggered back from the sheer power of my

voice. "Course not, Simon. You're as even-tempered as I ever seen you. Have been for the entire week. Ever since we saved Lizzie from that soddy, in fact."

"Got nothing to do with Lizzie," I snarled as I pushed past him. "Nothing whatsoever."

Lizzie turned out to have a few talents after all. She'd started in making tea for everybody from herbs and plants she'd been picking along the way. It was a soothing brew, and lucky to have, since our coffee supply seemed to have been guzzled away nearly unnoticed. There was also odd squares of sod now setting to dry all around the wagon and atop most of its bed. These was from a kind of sunken piece of land we'd camped next to, also unawares. Lizzie had noticed it this afternoon while Mr. Peece and I had had our words. She'd come over to say something; then she'd also noticed the plow sticking out of the corn, and the shovel.

"How smart of you, Mr. Peece!" she declared.

Just like that she said it. I caught the words from the patch of grass I was sulking behind.

"How wise to save my father's tools. He would have been happy that they didn't go to total waste after the effort he made to carry them West." She turned to that sunken patch. "And the shovel is just in time to dig some of this peat for our cook fires."

"Peat?" Mr. Peece tipped his hat from his brow questioningly.

"It makes excellent fuel. It burns a little smoky, but works nearly as well as buffalo chips."

I separated the blades of grass from before my face and peeked through. Lizzie did have a nice way of explaining things.

"And since buffalo chips seem to be a little scarce around here . . ." She walked to the wagon and reached inside for the shovel. "I think I'll just dig some peat. A few days of this dry heat and wind and it'll be perfectly usable."

"Let me!" I bounded from my hiding place. "Just show me where to dig, Lizzie. No point in you messing up your hands. No point whatsoever—"

"Simon!" Now she was frowning. "You won't let me walk the birds. You won't let me help set up camp. Just exactly how fragile do you think I am? Exactly how fragile could a person be to nurse six dying people? To slaughter the last of the animals when the food was gone to try to keep kith and kin alive a little longer?"

I wrestled the shovel from her. "You're doing just fine picking your plants and mending every stitch of clothing in sight," I said.

"With the sewing kit I wouldn't have had if you hadn't the sense to pack it in the carpetbag, Simon." She stopped, frustration written all over her body. "Just when are you going to allow me to function as a human being again? When are you going to stop protecting me?"

I almost spit out *never*, but managed to bite the word back in time. "You've got *ideas*, Lizzie. Ideas I couldn't ever have. It's a precious thing, that is. Like with this here peat business. Why don't you teach me how to harvest the stuff?"

Lizzie gave Mr. Peece a look, and I caught his shrug. Then she showed me how to dig peat.

❧ FIFTEEN ❧

The Smoky Hill Fork just used itself up and disappeared into a bone-dry channel of gravel. We had to take a chance and follow the rough trail the Pike's Peak or Bust gold rushers had carved into the prairie a couple of years back. It worked out fine when we met up with the Big Sandy Creek after about a half day's walk. The land started changing then, from straight-out flat to rolling. And at the end of another day's journey we had a new view.

"There they be," Bidwell Peece observed after he set the mules and horses to graze. He was standing by the wagon, sort of resting against it, gazing off to the west. "The Shining Mountains. The Rockies."

One by one, Jabeth and me and Lizzie wandered over to stand next to him. Lizzie carefully kept to the far side of Jabeth from me, like she'd been doing since that plow and peat business.

"They's nothin' but a haze of purple," Jabeth opined. "How far off you figure we are, Mr. Peece, sir?"

The drover rubbed his chin. "Round about a hundred miles, give or take a few. Won't be long now. Should make Denver inside of the week—all things bein' equal."

Only a week! I stole a glance at Lizzie. It weren't nearly long enough. Even if I knew there wasn't no future for me with her, it was still a comfort just being in the same vicinity. That would sure and certain stop come Denver. A lot of other things'd stop, too.

I studied Mr. Peece next. He'd trot off with his horses and his percentage to start up a new life. My head swung toward Jabeth. My friend would be gone, too. Not that we'd been quite the same ever since the grasshoppers and the soddy. Always seemed to take Lizzie's side, he did, like he was protecting her, too.

I looked up at the purple haze of mountains again. Those Rockies ran clear across the sky south to north, far as a body could see. They broke up the ocean of flatness I'd half believed would go on forever.

My eyes fell from the distance to my turkeys. They was already tucked up in their nests for the night, their bronze feathers blending into the sunset. They'd been good troopers all along. The best. I think they'd be content to keep walking as far as China if Mr. Peece and Emmett and I was to keep them company. What do you suppose was filling them tiny little bird brains now? Could they remember their river flight? And the camels? What about the soldiers? What about— I had to grin at the next thought, sure enough.

"What you smirkin' at, Simon?" Jabeth asked.

"Who, me? Nothing. Well, nothing much. Just wondering how long a turkey can remember the biggest grasshopper feast in all creation." I cogitated some more. "I figure maybe it's longer than a peacock could. I'm figuring maybe turkeys ain't as stupid as folks back in Union, Missouri, thought."

Mr. Peece chuckled. "Ain't none of us as stupid as all that, Simon."

Then the sun tucked down behind that purple haze, and Jabeth and Mr. Peece started shuffling away from the view. Somehow I ended up tarrying a moment longer, though. And somehow Lizzie Hardwick tarried with me. She played with the long braid all that fine hair was done up in. Just swung it over a shoulder and toyed with it.

"I'm sorry it's almost over, Simon. I was hoping we'd have time to become friends."

"But we *are* friends, Lizzie," I protested.

"What I mean is . . ." Her voice trailed off.

I leaned back into the wagon, feeling huge and gawky again, wondering where to set my feet, wondering what to do with my big paws. She didn't seem to notice, just kept staring toward the ridge of mountains, turning from purple to black now.

"That night . . . that night you stayed with me in the dugout?"

I muttered something unrecognizable. My throat was so tight it was all that would come out.

"You were my savior, Simon. My knight in shining armor. You'd come out of nowhere to slay the dragon of despair."

"Must've done an awful amount of reading in your time, Lizzie," I finally managed to croak out. "In your *sixteen* years." I cleared my throat. "To know about such things. To talk about them so pretty."

"We had books, yes. Before I burned them for tinder."

"*Sixteen* years' worth of books must make a mighty lot of tinder."

She flashed me an odd look. "I wasn't reading for all of my sixteen years, Simon."

"Still and all," I continued, "you must've been reading for a goodly number of those *sixteen* years, for to have such beautiful words in your head."

Lizzie stamped a foot. "What *is* it about you and sixteen years, Simon Green? If you say *sixteen* one more time, I'll, I'll—"

"You can do anything you want, Lizzie. Say anything you want. A *sixteen*-year-old young lady has got p'rogatives a fifteen-year-old boy ain't."

Lizzie screamed, furious and piercing. I clapped my hands over my ears as she marched on me. "There! Does that satisfy you? Or shall I scream again?"

Jabeth scrambled around the corner of the wagon, catching me with my arms still raised.

"What's happening? Anything wrong, Lizzie? You see a big old rattler or something?"

Lizzie yanked at her braid in frustration. "Nothing's wrong. Just go away, Jabeth." She watched his face fall and relented. "Please. Simon and I are only having a private discussion."

Jabeth slunk off and Lizzie turned on me again.

"That's what I have to put up with. From all of you! Treating me as if I'm some exotic creature on a pedestal! And you, Simon Green. You're the worst one of the lot. I'm sixteen years old and I want to be normal! I want to be treated normally. I want *you* to treat me normally!"

I was backing from her into the prairie as fast as I was able. Feeling strange, all hot and cold. "It ain't possible!"

"Why *ain't* it possible, Simon Green?" she yelled.

"Because, because—" I stumbled on a rock and collapsed onto a patch of drought-cracked earth—legs splayed out, flat on my bottom. Understanding the meaning of *despair* at last, I covered my face. The words still came forth, though. I couldn't stop them. They'd been bottled inside for what seemed an eternity. "Because I'm only *fifteen*. You're an older woman and couldn't ever have anything to do with me!"

There, it was finally out. I pulled my hands from my face and looked up to see what effect my confession had made on Lizzie. I had to stare hard through the darkening night sky. I shook my head and stared some more. Looked like she'd been taken right sudden with some sort of stomach ailment, the way she was bent over, clutching at her middle parts. Was it a left-over effect of the ague? Or had she been struck with the cholera? She never did say what her entire family had kicked the bucket over.

Cholera.

That had to be it. And here she was, the only woman I'd ever love, expiring before my very eyes.

"Lizzie!"

I leaped up to grab her, to comfort her, to give her the opportunity to die in the arms of someone who truly cared. Someone who would mourn for her forever. Someone who would trek back regular to plant flowers on her grave, even in this wilderness.

She was shaking when I touched her, right enough, but it weren't from any cholera. Lizzie Hardwick was convulsed with laughter.

"Simon Green!" she gasped out, tears streaming down her face. Then she let out a belly laugh like no other I'd ever heard. She must've been holding it in so that it hurt something fierce. "Simon Green, you great, hulking, blundering idiot!"

"What, Lizzie? What'd I do? I'll make it better, I swear to heaven—"

"You think a few months, or even a *year* makes any difference when two people have a feeling for each other?"

I dropped my hands from her and stepped back as her first batch of words registered. "Malign me all you want, Miss Lizzie. Won't be the first time in my life for that to happen."

She swiped at her face with the hem of her dress. The tears was still coming. "I'm not maligning you, you . . . you *turkey*-brained fool!"

That stopped me in my tracks. *Turkey*-brained had to be an improvement over *pea*-brained. From where I stood and the experiences I'd been through on this here great turkey walk, I'd have to admit to that point. Progress was being made.

She swiped at her face again. "I'm trying to tell you I *like* you, Simon. A whole lot."

Light began to dawn, slowly but surely. Even though the sun had only just set. "You mean to say it don't matter about you being *sixteen*—"

Lizzie's entire body went into those spasms again over that word. I soldiered on.

"—and me being *fifteen*?" I kept on plowing directly ahead. "Not to mention me being turkey-brained and all?"

Lizzie was sobbing now. I waited patiently for the sobs to settle. It took a while before she turned to me.

"You have more natural good sense—and goodness—than anyone I've ever met before in my entire life. Aside from this age business. Do you believe me, Simon?"

I scratched my head. "I guess so. And it's mighty nice of you to put it like that—"

"Come here, Simon," Lizzie ordered.

I edged closer.

"If you promise, solemnly promise, to treat me like a normal girl, you may give me a kiss."

I gulped. "I promise. I surely do, Lizzie. Cross my heart and hope to die."

"Good. But you can forget about the dying part." She pointed to her cheek. "Right here."

Well, I aimed for where she pointed, but I always was a little clumsy. Was it my fault it was her lips I found, instead?

"Simon! Lizzie?"

That was Mr. Peece's voice floating over the embrace.

"Your supper's sitting here waiting on you. And it's turning stone-cold!"

℘ SIXTEEN ℘

We found Denver at last. We kind of came at it roundabout, walking from the south along the Cherry Creek. As we got closer and closer to the mountains, I finally started fearing for my enterprise. Here we was with them Rockies poking up to high heaven nearly atop of us, and we hadn't come across anything like the amount of wagon traffic I'd been expecting. I'd begun to wonder if this boom town of Denver truly existed—not knowing then that all the movement into the place was coming from the north of us out of St. Joseph, along pieces of the Oregon Trail and the South Platte River.

Meanwhile, Emmett enjoyed Lizzie walking left flank with him those last few days. It'd taken him longer to sweeten up to her than with most people. Not that he barked or growled or anything of that nature. It was more like he was keeping his distance. Maybe deep in his doggy brain he connected her with that plague of grasshoppers he'd cowered under in some shame back on the flat plains. Once he'd decided there wouldn't be no more 'hoppers, though, he took to her training with energy.

"Emmett!" I heard Lizzie scold more than once. "You needn't nip at my heels. I can see that silly hen wandering off as well as you can!"

I'd set Lizzie to walking the birds as a part of our deal about treating her the same as a normal person. It was the lesser of two evils as I saw it. Jabeth—after he'd figured Lizzie and me was on comfortable terms again—had fixed his mind on training her to hunt with him.

"No way on this earth!" I squelched that one fast. I was still in charge, wasn't I?

"Why not, Simon? Hunting's a useful skill, and I got the feeling Lizzie would take real fine to a rifle."

"That might be so, and then again it mightn't." I stared Jabeth down. "Not that you've bagged anything more tasty than jackrabbits and rattlers lately. I'm getting mighty tired of rabbit and rattler stew."

"I can't shoot what ain't there, Simon. You knows that as well as me." He stared dejectedly around the rising foothills. "Unless you have a sudden taste for coyotes. They got them a bird last night."

"What? You didn't tell me about that!"

Jabeth scowled. "Felt too awful about it. There I was, sacked out in the middle of the flock's nesting ground, and I never heard a thing. Not a solitary howl."

"That's because you never hear *nothing* when you're sacked out, Jabeth. Could be an entire army of wolves and coyotes coming through." I stopped. No point in rubbing it in anymore. The losing, with us so close to Denver and market, was bad enough. "How'd you know, anyhow?"

"Found the empty nest this morning, with some speckles of blood. I tracked the trail of blood into the grass." He felt in his back pocket. "Here. It's all that was left."

I accepted the handful of shiny feathers and held them up to the sun. They was still a pretty bronze-green. "Maybe we'd better take turns keeping watch again tonight."

"Maybe we'd better."

But it worked out we didn't have to keep watch on account of coyotes that night—not the animal kind, at any rate. That was because that night we ended up in Denver. Leastways, on a rise right outside of it. The town was set on the flats below, directly to either side of where the Cherry Creek flowed into the South Platte. And Denver was already almost as big as Jefferson City!

We was all a little amazed as we settled the flock a final time. Here was the place we'd come for, right out of the blue. And we'd made it—with us and most of the birds intact. Mr. Peece had decreed the campsite, safely outside the town, still on the high plains with the Rocky Mountains another few miles to the west.

"We got to be on our guard from here on in, Simon," he said as he kept an eagle eye on where the birds was bedding down.

"So as not to be gulled?" I asked.

"Gulled—or worse." He took his time ungearing the mules. "We got to check out the inhabitants, work out a strategy. Won't be long before they spot the birds."

I glanced up from where he was working. Sure enough, people was already wandering out from the town to gawk at us. Mr. Peece noticed them—and that familiar hungry look—too.

"Jabeth?" he called. "Think it's time to break out the arsenal."

"The rifles?" Jabeth popped up. "Yes, *sir*, Mr. Peece!"

When I got to saunter into Denver at long last, I was taken aback all over again at how much like a city it looked. All laid out in neat squares it was, next to those two flowing strips of water. Day was fading fast, and as there weren't any lamplights to mention, I kind of hurried along with my survey through the dusty streets.

There was First Street, directly next to a bend of the South Platte River, and Front Street sidling up to Cherry Creek, with a wooden bridge to cross it. There was also a ferry to get to the other side of the Platte, and two churches—Methodist and Episcopal, which denominations seemed to have gotten here first—and rows of wooden buildings with painted signs and false fronts, to make them more impressive.

Wasn't an ounce of gold dust littering any of those streets, though, the way Mr. Buffey had claimed way back in Missouri. Even in the twilight, gold dust would've been hard to miss. That wasn't any big disappointment. I figured the gold would be more likely lurking in them fake-fronted establishments—at least, in the hands of their proprietors. Nobody in Missouri had ever met up with a prospector that'd returned with anything but more calluses on his hands.

So I took note right off of the provisioners, them that mined the miners. Next I registered a bank and a land office and a newspaper office and the express company. That express company, the Central Overland, California & Pike's Peak, had a big schedule posted out front. Couldn't believe my eyes when I read that their stagecoaches took both passengers and mail to and from Missouri every single day!

More or less satisfied, I ignored the saloons that was livening up for the night and headed on back to camp. I'd been worrying some about how to get a letter and money back to Miss Rogers once my birds was sold. Not to mention my debt to Uncle Lucas and Aunt Maybelle and the cousins. I hadn't thought of them in quite a while. Hadn't needed to. Wouldn't they be some kind of surprised when I come through the way I promised!

But the flock wasn't sold yet. Far from it. There was no point whatsoever in putting the cart before the horse. Not till the deed was done. Still, a genuine idea started growing in my head on the way back. Something Lizzie might be a help with.

After breakfast the next morning I sent Mr. Peece into Denver for a few supplies and arrangements I figured we might be needing for my idea to work. Also to get a feeling for the lay of the land himself. Bidwell Peece wasn't no birdbrain any way you looked at it, and I'd value his opinion added to mine. I sent Lizzie with him, too. She'd been jumpy with excitement over getting to see some civilization at long last, and I'd have to start trusting her out of my own sight sooner or later.

In the meantime, there was the turkeys to deal with. They'd gotten up bright and early like usual and started eyeing them mountains in the near distance as if they was more than game to take them on. I felt a little bad they wouldn't be getting a close look at the snow atop them Rockies, or China somewheres to the other side. In the here and now, howsomever, I had to convince them to stick around for a little enforced rest.

"Jabeth?"

"I'm right here, Simon."

Well, he was and he wasn't. Lizzie's herb tea hadn't seemed to waken him much this morning. Maybe that's on account of the fact that he'd spent a good piece of the night patrolling our camp with his favorite rifle, to make up for that coyote the night before. He was still hanging on to that rifle, stuck butt into the ground—maybe more like using it to prop him up.

"Might as well retire the weapon for now, Jabeth. We got to break out some corn for the birds before they decides to take on mountain-climbing."

"When do I get to see Denver, Simon? I got me an urge just as big as Lizzie's!"

"Soon," I promised. "Real soon, I hope."

Mr. Peece and Lizzie finally came back with a fresh supply of coffee beans. Mr. Peece set down the small sack reverently.

"Any idea what they're charging for food? For these here beans? You'd think *they* was gold—"

I didn't pay any mind to the man's grumbling. I was busy snatching at the sheet of paper that'd been fluttering from Lizzie's hands.

"Mr. Peece thought you'd like a copy as a sort of souvenir." She smiled. "They're being delivered to every business in town, and most of the houses, too, just the way you wanted it, Simon. Watch out for the ink! It's still damp—"

"Too late." I transferred a black smudge from my fingers to my pants. Then I smiled. "It turned out right nice, Lizzie. I knew you had a way with words!"

"They weren't all my words, Simon. Some were yours."

"But it was *your* idea from the start, Lizzie, these handbills—"

"But *you're* the one who knew newspaper offices did jobwork on the side, Simon—"

"Whatcha got there?" Jabeth struggled up from where he'd been napping in the shade of the wagon. "What'd I miss?"

"Only the final touch to our journey." I poked the sheet in front of his nose. *"The Rocky Mountain News* has a real nice way with print."

Jabeth frowned. "You know I can't read, Simon."

"You can't read?" I stared at him, dumbfounded. "I never knew that. Why, even *I* can read, Jabeth! What's the matter with you?"

"The matter is that nobody ever taught me! You think they got pretty little schoolhouses with pretty little schoolteachers like your Miss Rogers for *slaves?"*

"But you ain't a slave no more, Jabeth. Nohow."

"Still can't read, can I?"

"Well, well—"

"Read it for him now, Simon," Lizzie broke in. "And I can teach Jabeth how to read later. You can help me."

Later? *What* later, I wondered to myself. But I

didn't let on. "I can? I mean, sure and certain." I squared the damp sheet before my eyes. I cleared my throat. Lucky I already knew what it said, or my performance might've left something to be desired:

☞ **AUCTION!** ☜

HIGH NOON TOMORROW
BY THE CENTRAL CITY WELL

THE GREAT TURKEYS OF
THE GREAT TURKEY WALK!

Straight from Missouri, the finest, fattest, tenderest turkeys you ever set eyes on, or will ever sink your teeth into. They have arrived in Denver! Accept no imitations. Bronze turkeys are the best!

No scrip or shinplasters taken in payment. Gold coin only.

* * * *

Simon Green, *Proprietor of the flock*
Bidwell Peece, *Auctioneer*
Jabeth Ballou and Elizabeth Hardwick, *Facilitators*

Jabeth's brow wrinkled. "Mighty nice of you to put my name in print, Simon . . . But what in this wide world is a *fa-cil-i-ta-tor*?"

I turned to Lizzie. "Why don't you do the explaining? It being your word choice, same as that no-good paper money, the shinplaster business, was Mr. Peece's contribution."

Lizzie shrugged. "A facilitator is someone who helps the process along the way, Jabeth. Like you did by hunting and keeping everyone fed. I *told* Simon my name didn't belong there, next to yours, when you helped so much more, but he insisted—"

Jabeth graciously waved away Lizzie's protests. "No matter. I never been called a *fa-cil-i-ta-tor* before. It's a mighty fancy way of putting things. Mighty impressive." He shook the last traces of sleep from his body, and his shoulders took on their old jaunty swing. "Maybe I'll just go *fa-cil-i-tate* us a pot of fresh coffee."

Mr. Peece grinned at his back. "Good idea, Jabeth. Then we can all commence to making a proper count of our flock for tomorrow's auction."

I stared at Mr. Peece. That was the first time on the entire trip that he'd referred to the birds as *ours*. It made me feel good that everybody was truly getting excited about my enterprise the way they was. Too bad it was here at the very end of the line. Too bad we was all going to be broke up the same as my flock come noon tomorrow.

℮ SEVENTEEN ℮

My turkeys walked into Denver in high style the next morning. It was more as if they was doing a prancing kind of dance, really. They lifted their shiny brown claws high, and set them down again with rhythm—all the whiles they was bobbing their tiny purple-red heads and shifting their bright eyes right and left at the sights, wattles jiggling with excitement, gobbling and clicking to high heaven. I was that proud of them, with the brilliant sun glancing off their sharp beaks and gleaming feathers, that I sort of danced alongside.

And why not? Why shouldn't we all be proud? They was fulfilling their turkey destiny. They might end up as roasts soon, but they'd be the most famous roast turkeys ever. I'd done what I'd set out to do, too. I hardly noticed the folks of Denver lining the streets and cheering in high good humor as if we was a parade—as if we was *important*—I was so caught up in the accomplishment.

There was Mr. Peece, sitting high and purposeful on the wagon, urging Sparky and his brothers into a kind of fancy mulish high-step. The Arabian horses frolicked behind. Then came the birds, surrounded by Jabeth and Lizzie and Emmett, with me bringing up the rear. We'd all spruced ourselves up and donned our cleanest and best duds. I figured we'd worn the trail fairly well. But all good things come to an end. And the end was at hand as by and by we reached the open square around the city well.

From here on in, Mr. Peece was in charge—he being more of an authority figure than me anyways you looked at it. He took it in good stride, rising from his wagon seat to face the crowd gathering in all directions. He tipped his hat.

"Greetings, ladies and gentlemen, all good folks of the fine, forward city of Denver—"

He didn't get no further for a while, on account of those folks all started in cheering again. It wasn't clear whether it was the *good folks*, or *fine, forward city of Denver* part that set them up so, but as long as they was happy, I was happy. Mr. Peece finally got to start again.

"As you probably noticed in them broadsheets done up by your very own, most excellent *Rocky Mountain News*—"

More cheering cut in about then. Mr. Peece had to wave his hat around to calm things down.

"Anyhow, you noticed. And here we are, with the very birds promised. Nearly *one thousand* of the finest turkeys on this here continent—or any other. Walked over eight hundred miles strictly for your delectation." He paused to squint through the noon sun at the flock. "And tell me, folks. Have you ever seen a handsomer, healthier set of birds in your entire lives?"

Of course not. I joined in the cheering at that point. Ain't never *been* a better bunch of birds anywheres!

Mr. Peece grinned up a storm, then finally got down to business. "Glad we're agreed. Now, what do I hear for each head of turkey? What am I bid?"

"A buck a head!" somebody shouted.

"Sir!" Bidwell Peece turned downright sorrowful. "Sir! A mere dollar for these birds what've crossed countless rivers, what've crossed the vast, entire, great American prairie? For these birds that took on wild Indians and the complete U.S. Cavalry? Not to mention turkey rustlers! No sir, these birds has got a history to go with them. You set your teeth into one of these birds and you'll be swallowing the entire westward movement!"

"Two bucks a head!" yelled somebody else.

"When I paid near two bucks a bean for coffee only yesterday in your very shops?" Bidwell Peece's voice changed to scorn. "Come, come. We're talking thirty to forty pounds of luscious meat each!"

Mr. Peece went on that way for a while. The price

rose slowly. Mighty slowly, by nickels and dimes. Meantime, I'm standing there, sweating in the heat, wondering if this auction idea of mine had been a sound one after all. Wondering if I'd been a tad anticipatory in my five-dollar price. Sweating even more thinking on what was to happen if I didn't get that price—considering all the percentages I been promising left and right. Then somebody finally yells out the magic words.

"Five dollars the bird!"

I ran a dripping sleeve across my dripping brow. At last. I looked to Mr. Peece to make it a done deal. But Mr. Peece, he just stood up there on that wagon, waving his arms and talking a blue streak of nonsense. And the price goes up to five and a quarter. Then to five and a half. I'm sweating up a river about now. How far could Bidwell Peece truly go?

"I hear five-fifty. I've got five-fifty." He's chugging along like a steam locomotive. "Who'll go five-seventy-five? You, sir? I've got five-seventy-five. I'm bid five-seventy-five. Who'll go six bucks a head for the most incredible turkeys on the face of this earth?"

The crowd finally stilled. Mr. Peece searched every face in it. He built the silence. At last he singled out a little fellow sitting on the railing at the end of the block of buildings to one side of the square. A fellow smaller than Mr. Peece himself, perched so he could elevate himself to see above the crowd.

"You, sir. Amos Quinn, if I'm not mistaken. Are you not the proprietor of the fine provisions store where I purchased those fine coffee beans but yesterday morning? Those beans worth every cent I paid?"

He waited for the weak nod.

"Of course you are! Now think, Mr. Amos Quinn. Think what you can do with a flock of nearly *one thousand* turkeys in this great, turkey-hungry city of Denver!"

The little man pulled at the collar tightened around his skinny neck. He swallowed once or twice. A high squeak came forth. "Six dollars. That's my limit."

"Sol—"

Mr. Peece never got a chance to finish the end of the word. The word that was meant to change my entire future. That was because the Central Overland, California & Pike's Peak Express Company chose that moment to barrel through the crowd, the stagecoach's team of horses frothing at the bit.

"It's the stage from St. Joe!" someone shouted.

"Near forgot about its being due."

"Watch out for the turkeys!"

Watch out for the turkeys, indeed. In another instant my flock was about to be stomped flat into the ground. Destroyed before my very eyes. They couldn't fly, as there was no place to fly to, hemmed in as they already was by the crowd and the wagon.

Being at the rear of the birds, I did all that I *could*

do. I faced them frothing beasts, jumped right between the first set of harness, and wrestled the lead horses to a halt—about a yard in front of my worked-up birds. Next I glared up at the driver.

"Just rounded the corner, boy," he started to apologize. "Didn't expect no celebration here—"

By that time the door of the stage had sprung open. Out leaped a figure I'd been trying hard to forget. It was followed by another one I'd been hoping never to set eyes on again.

"Pa!" I gasped. "Cleaver!"

Pa was wearing a hat, which he never did. He was also carrying a revolver, which he shot into the air to get some attention. Not that he needed any more of that. Next he swept off the hat to give me a mocking bow.

Hadn't intended ever speaking to the man again, but I couldn't help it. The sight he'd revealed before my eyes was that unusual. He was clipped bald as an egg. "What happened to your fine head of hair, Pa?"

"Scalped! I been scalped! Or as near to as ever. Compliments of your peaceful Injuns, before Cleaver and me escaped again. Fine sense of humor they had."

Pa clamped the hat back over his shaved head and pushed his way through the turkeys, waving that pistol around. "Out of my way! I'm here to claim these birds as mine!"

Cleaver, also shorn like a sheep, followed. He was

holding *two* revolvers—one in each hand. "Any negotiating to be done gets done through us!"

"Why . . . why—" I spluttered. I turned to the good folks of Denver in appeal. My words flowed out. "Why, these is the selfsame turkey rustlers that's been dogging us every step of the journey! Twice already they tried to steal my birds!"

"The boy's a liar!" Pa yelled. "It's the other ways around."

Heads turned between the newcomers and me, beginning to wonder. I only stood there, my heart sunk about as low as it could sink. Luckily, other members of my enterprise was thinking more clearheaded. Emmett, the fastest, abandoned his precious flock long enough to leap straight up Cleaver's chest and bite into his nose.

Emmett got himself a good grip. He hung there by the teeth for dear life. Cleaver had to drop his guns to pound at him, but it didn't seem to have no effect. Meanwhile, Jabeth and Lizzie had disappeared into the rear of the wagon. In a moment they were out again, each aiming a rifle at Pa. Slowly the crowd decided to take sides.

"Ma! Why's that ugly, nasty man beatin' up on that poor little dog so?"

"I'm not certain, Emily, sweetheart, but I intend to put a stop to it."

I watched the lady march through the center of my

flock and bash Cleaver over his shiny pate with a parasol. Cleaver sank to the earth, Emmett still attached to his nose.

Then there we all stood—the good people of the forward city of Denver watching wide-eyed while my facilitators kept their weapons aimed steady at Pa and Cleaver. It looked to be another one of them stand-off situations until Mr. Peece blinked and spoke up again.

"Well, now." He swiped at his forehead. "Well, now, it seems like some explanations is due you good people. But first off we'll have to give you proof of our entire good faith. Especially to Mr. Amos Quinn here, who's just about to buy himself almost a thousand turkeys."

Mr. Peece stared over to where Mr. Quinn had been last seen. Seemed like he'd tried to make an escape from his commitments, because he was kicking and squirming in the hands of three good-natured louts.

"Still interested, Mr. Quinn?" Mr. Peece asked.

The louts grinned and shook him a few times. Amos Quinn managed to pipe up, "Proof! If you give me proof of legal ownership!"

Bidwell Peece turned to me. "Come on up, Simon, son. Let's straighten this out."

My birds and the people both opened up a path before me so's I could clamber up the wagon seat. There I sat down and methodically unlaced and removed my right boot. I pulled at the lining and poked underneath for what I hoped to heaven was still there. It was. I looked up. "Right here, Mr. Peece."

Further fishing brought forth a somewhat malodorous square of paper. I undid the folds, one by one, to flourish a full-sized sheet. The writing had gone a little weak, but it was still there, thank goodness. I read it out slowly and carefully.

" 'Sold to Simon Green, this Fifteenth Day of June, 1860. One thousand bronze turkeys.' " I looked straight out at the listening throng. "Signed, 'Uriah Buffey, of Union, Missouri.' " I sighed with relief as I turned to Mr. Peece. "Miss Rogers made me do that up. She sure and certain knew her business for a lady schoolteacher."

Mr. Peece patted my shoulder. "She sure and certain did, son." He squinted over the heads of the crowd at Amos Quinn. "Will that do, sir?"

Mr. Quinn nodded again, this time numbly.

"All right, then," Bidwell Peece yelled. *"Sold!"*

His nearly new black hat hit the dirt of the square.

"Sold to Mr. Amos Quinn of Quinn's Provisions and General Store! Nearly *one thousand* bronze turkeys! At *six dollars* the head!"

A moment of awed silence was followed by another cheer, this one the most raucous of them all. I paid no attention whatsoever as the cheerful crowd manhandled Pa and Cleaver off to the Denver jail for disturbing the peace, leaving Emmett behind to lick his chops. I edged off the wagon and sank down right there in the middle of my gobbling flock.

Me, Simon Green. I was a rich man.

We was back at our old camp overlooking Denver by early evening. It was a lot more quiet without nearly a thousand birds rustling around in the grass setting up nests. But not as quiet as all that. Emmett trotted up and plunked himself down on my lap. I scratched where he liked it.

"Reckon he's come to say thank you, Simon."

I glanced up at Mr. Peece. "How you figure that?"

"You saw how he near went crazy when Amos Quinn started taking off with the turkeys. Mighty nice of you to save a few for Emmett to look after."

I kept scratching the dog. I had been thinking of Emmett a little at that point, but of me, too. About how birds and me always got along so well. It suddenly had seemed a shame to end the relationship. "I only kept but the three toms and the thirty hens, Mr. Peece. And I don't know how long Emmett'll get to shepherd them."

Bidwell Peece leaned back into his bedroll next to the fire. To the other side, Lizzie was just about finished polishing the dishes. She'd taken to the job real industrious. That was after I'd presented her with the wedding-day daguerreotype of her parents that I'd stashed away in the corn for this last evening together. Jabeth was sprawled out next to me, blowing softly on that flute instrument of his. It was a peaceful scene, everybody sort of busy with their thoughts, yet comfortable with each other.

"That shepherding comment." Mr. Peece tugged off his hat and laid it down for the night. "What you meaning by that, Simon?"

I took in a breath and it sort of caught in my throat. "I'm meaning that the money's been all shared out, fair and square. And Miss Rogers's piece has been put aside. All them percentages you come on the walk for has been dealt with."

"And?" Mr. Peece drawled.

"And that means come morning you'll be heading off to make your new life, Mr. Peece. The way you planned." I looked around the circle of fire. "And Jabeth, he'll be free, freer than ever to start up *his* new life." I stopped at Lizzie. Like I said, we'd been comfortable with each other for the last hundred miles. But there hadn't been any more of those meetings behind the wagon. So there hadn't really been anything said about any kind of a future for her—or us. "And Lizzie'll probably want to settle down in Denver for the civilization—"

"Why don't you let Lizzie speak for herself?" she suddenly shot out, eyes flashing.

"Me too, for that matter." Mr. Peece reached behind his head. He hefted the sack of gold coins that was his share of the great turkey walk. Then he tossed it over to me.

"What's this?" I caught it, already almost knowing.

"My share of your next enterprise, Simon. If you'll have an old wreck like me around."

"On a permanent basis?" My eyes widened through the night.

"As permanent as the good Lord chooses, son."

"But, but—"

Another sack caught me in the ribs. I turned to Jabeth, rubbing.

"I want a part, too, Simon. Count me in."

Lizzie didn't toss her sack, which was much smaller, but was meant to be a help, nevertheless. She walked it over and put it in my hands.

"Tell me about your new enterprise, Simon. Please."

Well, first I laughed, then I had to swipe at my eyes. Finally I started talking, staring into the flames of the fire on account of I wasn't able to face their true affection head on just yet.

"I stopped in at the land office this afternoon. They got these claim clubs, for ranches, too. And the land we just finished walking through weren't bad at all for a little cattle grazing. Or turkey raising, either. And it's all available, thousands of acres of it . . ."

⸙ EIGHTEEN ⸙

When it was time to do the deed at last, Lizzie wrote down the words for me, just the way I said them. She didn't fix it up or make it fancy in any way. On account of how she said it ought to be pure me, Simon Green. Here's how the letter went:

Dear Miss Rogers,

I truly hope this finds you as I am, hale and hearty.

Well, I made it to Denver, just like you said I would. Mr. Peece and me and Emmett all made it fine. Along the way we also picked up Jabeth, met my long-lost pa and his no-good thieving gambler friend, Cleaver, and saved Lizzie from the godforsaken prairie. But what you're probably truly interested in hearing about is the turkeys. You'll never believe it, but they sold for *six* dollars the bird! The way I figure it, it comes out like this:

- 930 sold at $6, for $5,580
- 21 lost or stolen but paid back at $5, for $105
- 16 shot by U.S. Cavalry, eaten by coyotes, or given as a free-will gift to Pottawattomie (that's peaceful, hunting and farming Indians)
- 33 saved for my new flock

That comes to a grand total of $5,685, of which your 10 percent share works out to $568.50, plus the $250 I owe you for loaning me the money. It all adds up to $818.50, which I've rounded off to $820 'cause it's easier to work with. So I'm sending that back to you today, like I promised. I hope the stagecoach doesn't get held up by bandits or Comanche (the wild sort of Indians out here) or anything like that.

If you had the desire to write back to me—which I would truly admire—you can send something to "The Great Turkey Five Ranch" (that's in honor of Mr. Peece and me and Jabeth and Lizzie, and Emmett, also, on account of he worked his tail off the whole trip. Sparky and his brothers did, too, but mules don't seem to have no urge for immortality, as Mr. Peece keeps putting it). Send that to Denver, Kansas Territory, and they'll see I get it.

Your friend forever,
Simon Green

P.S. Lizzie is only *sixteen*, but talks every bit as nice as you already. Mr. Peece says Lizzie and me have to wait a year or two to find out if we really like each other the way we think we do. In the meantime, we're building as fast as we can to get up a ranchhouse and quarters for the livestock before the winter snows. It sure is nice Lizzie ain't on a pedestal anymore. Every hand we got is needed.

Author's Note
(or, It Really Happened!)

In the days before intercontinental railroads, highways, and trucking firms, the only way to get livestock on the hoof (or claw) to market was to walk it. Many have been the tales of great cattle drives. Hardly anyone remembers the great turkey walks, which required just as many heroics.

During the nineteenth century, feathered herds were routinely walked to Boston and other northeastern cities from surrounding farms. These treks, however, rarely covered more distance than fifty miles. The epic journeys took place in the West. In 1863 one enterprising gentleman actually walked a herd of five hundred turkeys from Missouri to Denver with only a wagon drawn by mules, the birds, and two boy drovers. Another entrepreneur of the period performed the same feat in reverse, walking a flock from California to the booming Comstock Lode of Carson City, Nevada, earning enough money to establish a famous cattle fortune. These intrepid pioneers were the inspiration for Simon and his enterprise.

Hist Fic

DATE DUE

FOLLETT